Trifling With Trouble

K.D. McCrite

Annie's®
AnniesFiction.com

Books in the Chocolate Shoppe Mysteries series

Library of Congress-in-Publication Data
Trifling With Trouble / by K.D. McCrite
p. cm.
I. Title
                    2018945964

AnniesFiction.com
(800) 282-6643
Chocolate Shoppe Mysteries™
Series Creator: Shari Lohner
Series Editor: Elizabeth Morrissey
Cover Illustrator: Bonnie Leick

10 11 12 13 14 | Printed in China | 9 8 7 6 5 4 3

That morning was not the first time Jillian Green had wished she could clone herself so she could be in two places at once.

She chopped onions with tears streaming down her face while her great-aunt, Cornelia Montgomery, sang "Oh Promise Me" for what must have been the twentieth time. Jillian had stopped counting at thirteen. It wasn't Cornelia's rather screeching soprano that bothered her, but the fact that the woman only knew the first few words and improvised the rest: "Oh promise me that someday, la de da da da dum de dum . . ."

Like a broken record, Cornelia started the refrain again.

"I think I'll run to the bakery and see if Bertie needs me. Sometimes we get a rush about now. I'd call her but she might be too busy to answer." Jillian set her knife down with a *thunk* and hurried to the sink. With the tap opened all the way, the water muffled Cornelia's voice a bit.

"If she doesn't, you hurry on back here so you can slice the cheese for the sandwiches." Cornelia glanced up from the broccoli florets she was breaking apart, eyes twinkling. Even at eighty-plus years old, her blue eyes were bright and clear. "Has preparing food for this anniversary party got you feeling romantic?"

"What? No."

"Seems to me you and Hunter are getting closer to the altar all the time."

Jillian had been dating Hunter Greyson, the handsome owner of Greyson & Sons Funeral Home, for a while now. There was no doubt they were serious, but Jillian wasn't quite sure they were to that point yet. She shook her head. "Actually, the activity of chopping onions has never led me down the garden path of romance."

"Don't be sassy." Cornelia shook a stalk of broccoli at her. "I'll sing at your wedding, if you want me to."

"You'll what?" Jillian suddenly felt queasy.

Cornelia held the broccoli like a microphone and launched into another rendition of "Oh Promise Me."

Jillian groaned. "I'll be back," she called over her shoulder as she fled out the back door to her white Prius. She drove straight to The Chocolate Shoppe Bakery with the air-conditioning on full blast to ward off the sweltering heat that characterized Georgia in July.

The bakery's warm, humid kitchen smelled of sugar, yeast, chocolate, lemon, and cinnamon. Combined, the flavors might have tasted unpalatable, but as fragrances, they blended together in a welcoming scent of home, family, and friends.

Bertie Harper, Jillian's grandmother and Cornelia's twin sister, raised her eyebrows. "What are you doing here? Surely you and Cornelia don't have everything done at Belle Haven, do you?"

"No," Jillian said, "but I thought I'd see if you and Lenora need any help with baking."

Lenora Ryan, Bertie's right-hand woman at the bakery, stepped away from the oven she was peering into and closed the door. She smiled at Jillian, her brown eyes carrying their usual warmth. "Honey, we got everything under control. I'll tell you the truth: One more body moving around in this hot kitchen will surely bake us all to crispy critters." The sweat glistening on Lenora's brow proved her point.

"She's right," Bertie said. "You go on home to Cornelia. We're on the last batch of cookies, and then I'm going to frost the cake. After that, we'll be ready for tomorrow."

Jillian cast a glance around at the bulging cooling racks

and shelves. She thought of the cool, efficient kitchen back at the mansion. Inside her head, she heard Cornelia singing like a broken record.

"Are you sure you don't want me here?" Had she tempered her plea with the right amount of nonchalance? She didn't want to come across as unwilling to assist her great-aunt.

Bertie's eyes took on a knowing expression. "What's Cornelia doing? Talking to Raymond, talking about Raymond, or asking Possum to talk to Raymond for her?"

"You know," Lenora said before Jillian could reply, "I'd take listening to that business about the cat and her poor deceased Raymond communicating with each other any day over this hot kitchen. Even her nonsense about the ghost of Virginia Belle flitting around somewhere or another in that big old house."

"Aunt Cornelia is singing," Jillian told them.

"Singing?" Bertie asked.

"Yep. 'Oh Promise Me.'"

"Mercy me." Lenora waved a hand as if waving away flies. "She might have had a passable voice at one time, but her tonsils screech like rusty hinges these days."

"Why, Lenora!" Bertie frowned.

Lenora fixed a stern gaze on Bertie. "And if you think your own whistling is any better, you ought to think again."

"My whistling? I do not whistle. My mother taught us it was tacky for girls to whistle."

"I don't care what you want to call it, but when someone puckers their lips and blows out a tune, I call it whistling."

"You're getting as bad as my sister—"

Lenora gaped past Jillian and Bertie. "Why, Wanda Jean Maplewood, what are you doing in our kitchen?"

Wanda Jean's luxuriant gray-and-white hair was usually caught up in a neat, thick bun, but it was currently sticking out around her face as if she'd been running a footrace—and losing. She flapped a piece of paper. "I'm taking care of last-minute items on Maudie's to-do list."

Bertie frowned. "Don't tell me she's changed her mind about the food, because we have it all finished except—"

"She needs a few loaves of gluten-free bread."

"That's it?" Bertie asked.

Wanda Jean tucked a tendril behind one ear. "Right. She said two or three loaves ought to do it."

Lenora huffed. "Why didn't she say something about this earlier?"

"I reckon she didn't know she needed them," Wanda Jean said. "It's not a problem, is it?"

"If someone has an intolerance to gluten, it's a problem for them," Jillian said. "But she isn't expecting a whole array of gluten-free snacks, is she?"

"No. She doesn't want to create any trouble. It's just that . . ." A sly smile formed on Wanda Jean's lips. She came farther into the room and lowered her voice. "She didn't know her, um, surprise guest had this condition." She wriggled her eyebrows in a clear indication she had more to say but wanted to be coaxed into sharing.

Jillian didn't encourage the woman to tell all, although she was mildly curious about the "surprise guest." Harboring every confidence that Wanda Jean, one of the two biggest gossips in Moss Hollow, would impart her secret without encouragement from any of them, she started toward the door. "Since you don't need me here, I'll get back to Cornelia."

"Hugh Honeycutt's gonna get his socks knocked off tomorrow," Wanda Jean hinted. Hugh was Maudie's husband, and the event that required so much food was their fiftieth wedding anniversary party. The celebration was being held the next day in the Honeycutts' backyard, with food provided by some of Maudie's friends in the

Southern Sweetie Pies baking club.

"Oh?" Bertie said. "I hope he enjoys that. I'm not fond of having my socks knocked off."

Wanda Jean huffed. "I declare, if you were going to see your brother, whom you've not seen in more than fifty years, I bet you wouldn't mind the shock one little bit." She smoothed her messy hair with one hand.

"Say what?" Lenora said.

Jillian stopped at the door and turned back. "Brother?"

Wanda Jean nodded. "Yes."

"I didn't know Hugh had a brother," Bertie said. "Did you, Lenora?"

"First I ever heard of it."

"Apparently no one knew except Hugh himself." Wanda Jean was clearly getting into her groove now that she had everyone's interest piqued. "Maudie didn't know a thing about it until she was going through a box of things in the attic a few weeks ago. She found an old newspaper article about Farris Honeycutt coming in second to his younger brother, Hugh, in a regional track meet back when they were in high school."

"Forevermore!" Bertie said. "A brother. Why don't we know anything about him?"

Wanda Jean shrugged. "No one knows but Hugh."

"Wait a minute," Jillian said. "Wouldn't any of you remember him when he was a boy? If he was some kind of athlete, wouldn't he be pretty popular in town? After all, Moss Hollow isn't exactly a big city."

"It's not even a little city," Lenora declared.

"Hugh didn't grow up here," Bertie said. "I think he's from Missouri. He and Maudie met while she was on vacation with her folks in St. Louis."

"That's right. They met in early June and got married in late July."

"Of the same year?" Jillian could hardly believe the rather sensible Maudie Honeycutt would do something that impulsive and romantic.

"Yep. Love at first sight." Wanda Jean's smile went soft and wistful. "She brought him here right after the ceremony, and they set up house over in that little place near the elementary school. While she worked, he built the house where they live now. That was the first house he built, you know."

"I didn't know that," Jillian said, "but I know he built houses for a living."

"Hundreds of them in Nathan County," Bertie said.

"It would be nice if he was still building them," Lenora put in. "He did quality work, not these throw-'em-together-in-a-couple-of-weeks kind of houses that are being put up these days." She sighed. "But some folks like retirement. I reckon Hugh is one of them. And goodness knows he's earned it."

"Gives him time to watch baseball." Wanda Jean tucked up a stray lock of hair into her bun and secured it with a bobby pin. "Maudie says he watches every single game he can in the summer. In the winter, he watches some channel that broadcasts reruns."

"Reruns of baseball games?" Bertie shook her head. "Now that's got to be dull."

Wanda Jean shrugged. "Not for him, apparently. He enjoys it. All day long, every day. He passed the obsession on to Cameron too."

"Doesn't Cameron have a job in the major leagues?" Lenora asked.

"He's a talent scout," Wanda Jean said. "And it's a busy season for him. He and Iris and their boys won't be able to come to the party because he's traveling too much."

"That's a shame," Jillian said. "I'm sure Maudie is disappointed their only son can't come to their golden anniversary party."

Wanda Jean waved a dismissive hand. "She doesn't seem too sad about it. She and Hugh are planning a visit out to California to see them in October."

"What about the dogs?" Jillian asked. "I can't imagine they'd leave them behind."

"Maudie is going to interview dog sitters, then hire one to stay at the house the entire time she and Hugh are gone." Wanda Jean let out a laugh. "Can you believe that? No kennel for Mosey and Ambler."

Lenora chuckled. "I get a kick out of the way they baby their dogs. Probably let them sleep right in the bed with them."

Bertie met Jillian's eyes and they shared a grin. Possum, the pampered cat at Belle Haven, couldn't be more spoiled if he'd been a baby. He received a steady supply of bacon and often slept at Cornelia's feet.

"Seeing his brother again will be a big surprise for Hugh, if . . ." Wanda Jean trailed off again.

"If what?" Bertie asked irritably.

"If word doesn't get around."

"We're not going to tell anyone," Jillian assured her.

"I don't have time to tell anyone," Bertie said.

"And I don't want to tell anyone," Lenora said, then added, "although it sounds to me like it might not be such a great surprise."

A frown sliced into Wanda Jean's forehead. "What's that supposed to mean?"

"If there has been no communication between these two men since before Hugh and Maudie got married, there's bound to be a reason."

"I agree," Bertie said. "I don't think springing this surprise on Hugh is a good idea."

Wanda Jean planted her hands on her hips. "That's about the most shortsighted thing I've ever heard. Why, Farris has agreed to come, so if he's willing to show up, surely Hugh will be happy to see him again."

"I wouldn't be so sure," Jillian murmured.

Wanda Jean pinned a glare on her. "Oh, really? So you think it's okay for brothers to be estranged their entire lives?"

"No, but I don't know the reason behind that estrangement," Jillian said. "If something happened that was significant enough to keep them apart for over five decades, then chances are good that they don't want to see each other again. And it seems to me that this surprise reunion shouldn't happen at a party, in front of a lot of people."

"Well, I'm glad I don't have your cold heart," Wanda Jean said with a sniff. "Maudie is trying to bring them together before it's too late, and I applaud her for that." She glowered at Jillian again before turning to Bertie. "Thank you for agreeing to make the gluten-free bread. Apparently, Farris's wife is intolerant. To gluten, I mean." She glanced down at the list in her hand and her expression changed to one of dismay. "I have so much to get done. See y'all at the party tomorrow evening."

The three women watched her go, then Lenora said, in her usual blunt and down-to-earth way, "If Maudie wanted to keep that reveal a secret, she has already told it to the wrong person."

"**W**hat are we supposed to wear to Maudie and Hugh's party tomorrow night?" Savannah Cantrell Wilson asked Jillian on the phone that evening.

Jillian was sitting on her bed, legs stretched out straight and unmoving, toes splayed while cherry-red polish dried on the nails. Although her best friend had recently gotten married, the women kept in close contact, frequently calling each other at night, just as they'd done when they were girls.

"Since it's an outdoor buffet, I'm thinking casual. If Maudie had wanted a dressy affair, she would have booked a more formal venue, like the country club over in Bristow. A backyard bash in the summer doesn't sound like an occasion for sport coats and high heels."

"James has a pair of Bermuda shorts he wore on our honeymoon, but we didn't know anyone in Aruba. I'm not sure Moss Hollow is ready for the sight of his legs."

"Skinny and pale?"

"Exactly, but I did not say that."

Jillian giggled with Savannah. She waved one foot back and forth, hoping to dry her nails faster. "I heard they've hired a band from Painter's Ridge."

"Good thing the Honeycutts' backyard is so large. Thankfully all those trees will provide plenty of shade. Maybe there'll be a breeze after sundown."

Jillian thought about what Wanda Jean had said earlier that day in the bakery. She and Savannah rarely kept secrets from each other, and she yearned to share the disconcerting news, but she'd given Wanda Jean a promise to say nothing.

"Do you think this mysterious guest Maudie invited might be a celebrity?" Savannah asked.

Jillian startled a little at Savannah's question. She was sure both Lenora and her grandmother had held their silence. "How'd you find out about that?"

"Find out about what?"

"A mysterious guest."

"A couple of people mentioned it today. I forget who it was." There was a long pause before Savannah spoke. "Jillian, what do you know about this? I can sense it in your phone voice."

"My phone voice?"

"It's the funny little squeak you get in the back of your throat when you're trying hard to be casual."

"I do not squeak."

"You do. Like a mouse. I bet if I were over there right now, I'd see you rubbing your throat as if you're choking on words."

Jillian dropped her hand to her lap and sat straight up. "I am not."

"Uh-huh. So what can you tell me about this surprise?"

"Nothing."

"Jillian."

She huffed. "I promised not to say anything."

"Oh? And to whom did you make this promise?"

"Savannah Wilson, are you trying to wring gossip out of me?"

"Of course I am. Is it working?"

"I'd love to tell you what I know because it's something that has me concerned. But I made a promise."

"Jillian, everyone knows that when you promise to keep a secret, your best friend doesn't count. But if you still don't want to talk about it, we are definitely going to discuss it first thing after the secret is revealed."

"I'd die if we couldn't."

"I wouldn't want that," Savannah said with laugh. "I'll see you tomorrow evening then."

As she ended the call, Jillian couldn't help but wonder if everyone in Moss Hollow knew about the Honeycutts' mystery guest. If so, maybe Hugh wouldn't be so unsuspecting, after all.

"You're going to the party with Hunter, aren't you?" Cornelia asked late the next afternoon as they packed up the party food. Maggie, The Chocolate Shoppe's countergirl, would drive the bakery van to Belle Haven to help load and then deliver everything to the Honeycutts' residence.

"I am." Jillian smiled as she thought of spending the evening with Hunter. He was kind, gentle, and decent. His sense of humor brought laughter to her lips, and his compassion warmed her soul. No other man she'd ever met gave her the same settled feeling Hunter instilled. Trust was important to Jillian. She'd been stung hard by her ex-fiancé, David Drake, to whom she'd been engaged when she lived in California. She had believed him to be a solid, good-hearted, successful man. Instead, he'd turned out to be a sneak and an embezzler. Too bad she hadn't seen through him before they got together. She comforted herself by being glad he'd been caught before they were married.

Once the food had been loaded into the van, Jillian hurried upstairs to shower and dress for the party. She chose a classic white sundress sprigged with small red roses and wide shoulder straps. She pinned her wayward red hair up into a loose knot and arranged a few wisps to frame her face. A pair of white sandals that showed off her freshly painted toes completed the outfit.

Hunter arrived a few minutes later, and, after exchanging a few pleasantries with Bertie and Cornelia, he and Jillian left in his dark silver Lexus.

"Oh no," he said as they drove away from Belle Haven. "I was so eager to pick you up that I walked off and left my gift on my dining room table. I hope you don't mind if we detour to my place so I can pick it up."

"But that's what's in here." She picked up the gold gift bag containing the handmade quilt they had bought together at a local festival.

"I have something to add to that." His eyes twinkled.

She grinned at him. "Aren't you a sly one? Don't make me guess, Hunter. What is it?"

"A pair of Braves baseball jerseys that have 'His' and 'Hers' on them where the last names would usually be."

Jillian giggled. "They'll love them. I bet no one else thought of something like that."

"I put both our names on the card."

"Aww." She leaned across the space that separated them and kissed his cheek. "You're terrific, you know."

"I try."

It took a few minutes to drive across town to Hunter's place and retrieve the gift. By the time they reached the Honeycutts' street, it was lined with partygoers' cars. Hunter had to park a ways down the block from Hugh and Maudie's neat white bungalow.

"Who do you suppose the mystery guest is?" he asked as they walked toward the house.

Jillian shot him a glance. *So he's heard about Maudie's "secret" too.* At least he didn't know everything. "We'll find out soon enough."

Music from the 1960s throbbed through the evening air as

the pair made their way toward the back.

"I didn't expect Beach Boys songs at this party," Jillian said.

He gave her a quizzical smile. "What did you expect? Hip-hop?"

She chuckled. "No, definitely not hip-hop."

He took her hand, and they joined the party. The air was scented with the aroma of freshly mowed grass and was laden with laughter and chatter. Clusters of gold-tinted balloons bobbed gently in the early evening light, and solar lamps and colorful paper lanterns had been scattered throughout to offer illumination after the sun went down. The band played on a small platform in one corner of the yard. Everyone was dressed in casual summer clothes, just as Jillian had predicted.

On the lawn, a large table held the food prepared by Lenora and the Belle Haven women. Another table held urns of coffee, sweet tea, lemonade, and fruit punch, as well as an ice bucket, paper cups, and plastic tumblers. Between the two longer tables, a small round pedestal was topped with a three-tiered white cake that resembled a wedding cake. Gold ribbon encircled each tier, and a golden *50* ornament was set on top. Jillian knew that it was Bertie's famous coconut cake, and she couldn't wait to dig into a piece.

Cornelia, Bertie, and Lenora lingered nearby, ready to serve. They'd worked hard the last two days preparing for this party, and Jillian knew they were tired. Watching the crowd, Jillian was afraid the busy evening would take its toll on those three dear women.

"I should stay here and help with the food," she told Hunter.

Bertie overheard and favored her with a disproving expression. "You most certainly should not. This is self-serve, and these folks are plenty able to help themselves. We're here to replenish anything as needed and have fun."

"That's right. We have this under control," Cornelia added.

Lenora made a shooing gesture. "We'll call you if we need you. But we won't need you."

"Go on now," Bertie said. "Enjoy yourselves."

"You're sure?"

"I'll put you on cleanup detail all by yourself if you don't go now." Bertie aimed a pointed glare at Hunter, who was standing behind her. "Take that girl away from here before I decide she can't have a slice of my coconut cake."

He chuckled. "Yes ma'am." He tucked one hand in the crook of Jillian's arm. "Don't make a fuss," he told her. "You wouldn't want to miss out on that cake." He led her away from the now-beaming trio.

They added their presents to the table piled high with flowers, gift bags, and wrapped gifts. Wanda Jean was peering into bags and shaking the wrapped presents.

"Anything for me?" Hunter asked with a grin. "Or you?"

Wanda Jean glanced up and appeared to be completely unembarrassed to be caught snooping. "I haven't seen our names on anything yet. But it looks like they got plenty of nice presents. One thing I can't figure out, though." She pointed to a large gift that was wrapped in red-and-white-striped paper and tied with sparkly green ribbon. "Did Santa Claus get his days mixed up?"

"Maybe it's a fruitcake," Jillian joked.

"Mighty big fruitcake, if so." Wanda Jean laughed with them, her face relaxed and rosy.

"I'm sure Maudie appreciated your help in getting this party arranged," Hunter said. "You did a great job."

"Thank you. It wasn't easy. We're not as young as we used to be, and it's been plenty hot." Wanda Jean fanned her face with her hand. "I'm glad she and Hugh don't have a golden anniversary every year. I'm plumb worn out."

"You don't look worn out. You look lovely," Hunter said.

Her cheeks pinkened and she gave him a smile. "Why, thank you, Hunter."

Wanda Jean rearranged a few of the packages so they were more neatly positioned on the table, then began chatting with a newly arrived woman who added a narrow gift wrapped in metallic paper.

"It was sweet of you to compliment her," Jillian said as they walked away.

"Wanda Jean is a lovely woman, and she has some fine qualities. It doesn't hurt to let people know you've noticed them. By the way, have I told you that you look beautiful in that dress?"

She grinned at him. "Thank you. And so do you. Look handsome, I mean."

"What, this old thing?" Hunter gestured to his khakis and polo shirt, making Jillian chuckle. "Let's go congratulate the bride and groom while we're both so attractive."

Jillian glanced around the crowd. Near the beverage table, Maudie stood next to a tall, thin woman in aqua capris and a matching sleeveless silk top. Strappy high heels glittered on her feet and displayed her bright coral toenails. Her dark hair was in an extremely short blunt cut with heavy bangs. Huge sunglasses hid her eyes.

Maudie's smile seemed forced as she nodded and chatted with the woman.

"Do you see Hugh?" Jillian asked Hunter.

He shook his head. "Maybe he went to get more ice or something. There never seems to be enough ice at outdoor parties." He took her hand as they walked toward Maudie. "Do you know that woman with her?"

"I've never seen her before."

"Jillian and Hunter," Maudie said as they approached, "I'm so glad you made it."

"We wouldn't have missed it for the world," Jillian said.

"Congratulations, Maudie," Hunter said. "Fifty years of marriage is a remarkable milestone."

"It sure is. Thank you. And thank you for coming this evening." The relief in her voice was unmistakable. She leaned forward, gave each one a quick hug, then introduced them to the woman beside her. "This is Starla Higgins, Hugh's cousin from Phoenix."

"It's nice to meet you." Starla offered a tight smile, which folded her sunbaked face into a virtual spider's web of wrinkles. Her voice was neither warm nor chilly, and since Jillian couldn't see her eyes behind the dark lenses, she was unsure if the woman was looking at her, at Hunter, or at something else entirely.

"I hope you had a nice trip to Moss Hollow," Jillian said.

"Quite a pleasant flight to Atlanta, thank you." Starla turned to Maudie. "I'm going to see if I can find that husband of yours. I flew across the country to visit with him, not the locals." She touched Jillian's shoulder briefly with her lacquered fingertips as she passed. "No offense."

"I can't imagine where he went," Maudie said. "When you see him, would you please tell him that I need him immediately?" She cast an uneasy glance around the yard.

"Certainly."

Hunter followed Maudie's gaze across the guests and their surroundings. "How long has Hugh been gone?"

"I'm not quite sure. The last I saw of him was right after Starla and Sheldon arrived. That was a couple of hours ago." Maudie swallowed hard. "I've greeted our guests alone, and I shouldn't have to do that when it's a golden wedding anniversary party."

"No, you shouldn't," Jillian said firmly.

"And I'm all but at the end of my wits and patience. Wanda Jean is supposed to make sure everyone knows about the food and drink, but she seems more interested in visiting than helping. Not that I don't appreciate how much time and effort she has extended in lending me a hand to put this party together. Hugh didn't help at all, believe it or not. He's more interested in the countdown to the playoffs. The World Series is still months away, you know."

She didn't disguise the bitter tone in her voice, which bothered Jillian. Usually, if Maudie made remarks about her husband, they were either supportive or humorous.

"Try not to worry," Jillian said. "We'll help you. Hunter, would you please stay here with Maudie while I go find Hugh?"

He smiled warmly at the older woman. "I would be honored to greet the guests with you, if you're agreeable."

"Of course." She gave him a grateful smile. "And, Jillian, if you don't mind looking for him, I'd be ever so thankful."

"I'm happy to do it. You just keep smiling and chatting, and act like nothing is wrong, since I'm sure nothing is. Hunter is a great one to help distract a person from their worries." When Hunter lifted one eyebrow, Jillian added, "You are, and you know it. I'll be back soon."

Jillian worked her way through the guests, pausing only long enough to greet or exchange a few words, always keeping her eyes open for Hugh's tall, white-haired figure.

She moved from the crowd in the backyard to the neatly manicured front yard. Gift-bearing guests continued to arrive, coming along the sidewalk from both directions, smiling and talking to one another. They were all known to Jillian, and each of them paused long enough to exchange a greeting and a few pleasantries before moving on to the backyard. She wanted to ask them if they'd seen Hugh, but she knew her inquiries might rouse speculations. The less fodder for gossip the better, especially when it had to do with someone's long and supposedly happy marriage.

It was early dusk with a slight breeze, so maybe Hugh had

decided to take a walk in the neighborhood. But as soon as the idea formed, she questioned it. Who would leave their own party to take a walk? That would be rude. On the other hand, he *had* left his own party. So, rude or not, he was absent, and his wife was upset.

Maybe he found out that his brother was coming and couldn't face him.

That idea reawakened other questions, such as why they were estranged in the first place, why they hadn't ever reconciled, and whether they had ever attempted and failed to make up.

Then again, the meanderings of her mind might be completely off track. Why, Hugh might have gone—

The vehicle approaching tooted its horn, startling her. She turned to see Hugh waving and grinning at her from the driver's seat of his red pickup.

He pulled even with her, slid down his window, and called out cheerfully, "The party is back that way." He pointed toward his house.

Jillian glanced both ways, then trotted across the street to speak to him through the open window. "Good grief, Hugh, where have you been? Maudie is worried sick."

His smile slipped a little. "I didn't mean to be gone this long."

"Why didn't you call?"

"Because she would've asked a lot of questions that I wouldn't have wanted to answer." He gave her a lopsided grin. "I went to pick up her anniversary present, and at the last minute decided to get two instead of one, so I had to wait for shots and a bath."

"What?" Jillian couldn't fathom what sort of gift Hugh was talking about.

"It took longer than I expected. Look." He turned and reached into a large box on the floor of the passenger's side. "This one is Trudy, and this one is Roscoe." He held up two chubby, fuzzy, wriggling golden-haired puppies. One wore a blue collar and the other a pink one.

"Oh my goodness." Jillian's annoyance evaporated, and her heart turned as gooey as a marshmallow. She took the one with the pink collar and was rewarded by a tiny, overeager tongue wetting her nose, cheek, and chin. "They are the cutest things ever!"

Hugh chuckled. "I know it. Maudie has been saying for several months how she'd like to have a goldendoodle."

"Goldendoodle?"

"A crossbreed between a poodle and a golden retriever. A lady in Howard County raises them. I'd put a hold on Roscoe a couple of weeks ago, but today, when I saw how close he and Trudy were, I just couldn't separate them, so I took them both. That's why I was gone longer than expected. It took the lady a while to get Trudy all spiffed up to meet her new mama."

"Maudie will adore them."

"You know how much Maudie loves dogs."

"I do know that." Jillian handed Trudy back. "But, Hugh, she's none too happy with you right now. If I were you, I'd hightail it to the party."

"A little miffed, is she?"

"You could say that."

He started the pickup rolling forward. "Thanks for the warning."

Jillian hurried back down the street to rejoin the celebration. Savannah and James, who had opted for khakis like Hunter instead of the Bermuda shorts Savannah had mentioned, stood near Hunter and Maudie, so she joined them.

A few minutes later, Hugh came out into the backyard carrying a large box sporting a huge gold bow. He wore a big grin, but he looked a little nervous as he approached his wife. Everyone quieted as they watched.

"My goodness, I thought you'd run off." Maudie's laugh didn't sound as forced as it probably was. She had enough class not to display her aggravation with Hugh in front of their guests.

"I ran off, but not for reasons you might suspect," he teased, wriggling his eyebrows. "I went to pick up your anniversary gift, and it wasn't quite ready."

Her eyebrows shot up. "Oh?"

"What is it? What did you get her?" Wanda Jean pushed her way to the front of the crowd.

Savannah grabbed Jillian's forearm and whispered, "If Maudie doesn't open that box right away, Wanda Jean will do it for her."

Jillian suppressed a giggle.

"Open your present, Maudie," Hugh said. "I'll hold onto it for you."

She eyed him a moment, and a small mutinous light gleamed in her eyes. "Just set it on the table with the other gifts, and we'll open them all at the same time."

A frown shot across his face. "It'd be better to open this one now."

"But I want to wait—"

"Maudie, I think you should open it now." Jillian gestured encouragingly. "Go ahead."

"If you don't, I will," Wanda Jean said.

"Told you so," Savannah murmured to Jillian.

One of the puppies whined, a high-pitched mewling sound that wasn't easily identifiable.

Savannah stiffened. "Do I hear a baby crying?"

"In a manner of speaking," Jillian said.

"What's that supposed to mean?"

Jillian smiled. "Wait and see."

Savannah narrowed her eyes. "What's going on? Does this involve the mystery guest?"

Jillian had momentarily forgotten about the guest who had yet to be revealed to everyone. When it happened, she hoped Hugh would look as happy as he did right then, watching his wife untie the ribbon on her surprise.

"Hurry up!" Wanda Jean screeched.

Maudie stopped and turned to her best friend. "Wanda, please. You are making me tense."

Wanda Jean crossed her arms and huffed. "I bet you're a real hoot on Christmas morning."

A tittering laugh and a few murmurs passed through the crowd.

"This is the way she unwraps gifts," Hugh told them. "Tearing neither tape nor paper. And she saves the paper."

"We'll be here all night," someone called out, and everyone erupted into laughter.

"The longer you all holler at me," Maudie said in her most contrary voice, "the longer it'll take me to open this."

"Everybody hush." Wanda Jean passed a stern gaze around the group, which only served to create more snorts of laughter.

"Wanda, take this ribbon, please." Maudie handed it over, then lifted the top off the box. She peered inside, her eyes getting larger and larger, then a huge grin split her face. "Oh. My. Goodness. Hugh, what on earth?"

Wanda Jean was at her side in less than a heartbeat, gawking into the box with her.

"What is it?" several people called out.

Maudie reached inside and pulled out Roscoe and Trudy. Both puppies snuggled into her chest as if stunned by the excitement surrounding them.

"Don't they have a dog already?" Hunter asked Jillian in a low voice.

She nodded. "Two basset hounds, Mosey and Ambler. Grace, the shar-pei, died last year of old age. The Honeycutts are going have a houseful of dogs."

He chuckled. "They sure will, but if anyone can handle four

dogs in the house, it's Maudie."

Maudie's face was alight with joy and surprise. "Oh, Hugh, you darling, darling man!"

"Am I forgiven for being late?"

"Yes, you are." They leaned toward each other and shared a quick kiss while the others applauded and called out congratulations. "And here comes my gift for you." She dipped her head to something beyond him. "Come on, you two. Make your presence known."

Hugh turned with a big grin to see his gift.

Jillian held her breath.

A tall man Jillian had never seen before strode through the crowd. A smiling dumpling of a woman, who wore her platinum hair in a long braid all the way down her back, followed a step or two behind, eyeing everyone and waving at the crowd as if they were a renowned couple meeting their public.

The man resembled Hugh in build and coloring, and a huge smile was spread across his weathered face. "Happy anniversary, Hugh!"

Hugh's gleeful expression slid away, replaced by shock. The empty box he held slipped from his grasp and hit the ground.

"What's the matter?" the man asked, still grinning. "You look like you've seen a ghost. Don't you recognize your own brother?"

Hugh's gaze shifted to the woman who lingered just behind Farris. She offered a coy smile and delicate little wave. The festive atmosphere around them changed and everyone grew still. A dark flush stole up Hugh's neck, and his nostrils pinched as he took in a hard breath.

"Hugh?" Maudie said. The puppies in her arms whimpered and nuzzled the buttons of her blouse.

Hugh clenched and unclenched both hands, and Jillian thought he surely was about to punch the other man.

His brother thrust out his right hand, his face questioning, a little troubled. "Don't you have anything to say?"

"Farris, I do believe your brother is completely flummoxed, because he's never at a loss for words." Maudie nudged her husband with her shoulder as the puppies squirmed. "Honey, this is my anniversary present for you. It took a lot of doing, but I finally located your long-lost brother. I asked him and Della to come for a visit. I bet you didn't even know you have a sister-in-law, did you? Isn't it wonderful that they're here?"

Hugh slowly turned his head and gazed at his wife. There was something in his eyes and on his face that Jillian couldn't quite identify. The word "flummoxed" might have been too mild a description.

"I gave you two puppies that you've been wanting for a long time, Maudie," he said softly. "Even though we don't need more dogs, I knew how much you wanted a goldendoodle."

She gave him a puzzled look and an uncertain smile. "Yes, honey, and I love them. Thank you so much." She gave each pup a kiss on the top of its head. "And I brought your brother to you, all the way from Wyoming. Aren't you pleased about that? Haven't you missed him?"

Hugh's glassy-eyed stare never flickered from her face.

"C'mon, little brother. The past is behind us. Forgive and forget, what do you say?" Farris held out his hand again.

Hugh finally turned from his wife and regarded Farris's proffered hand.

"C'mon," Farris urged, closing in one more step.

As if he were nothing more than a husk without purpose, Hugh shook the man's hand. His smile was nonexistent.

"Me too?" The woman, Della, stepped into full view as she held out her right hand, which was practically dripping with silver rings. Instead of shaking hands with him, though, she pulled him toward her and gave him a huge hug. The chunky necklace she wore produced a clanking sound as it hit the buttons on his polo shirt. She planted a kiss on his pale cheek. "Oh, Hugh, I have missed you so much. We both have." She released him. "Haven't we, Farris?"

"We sure have."

Hugh stepped back. "Wyoming, eh?"

"We have a small ranch," Farris said. "You'll have to come see it."

"You'll love it, Hugh," Della said, clapping her small hands together and producing more jewelry clanking.

At the sound, Hugh seemed to come out of a stupor at last. He turned from Farris and Della and sent a glance around the other guests.

"I thought this was supposed to be a party, y'all. Let's get back to the fun."

With his words, the tense atmosphere began to ease and everyone else started moving away. He glanced at his relatives. "Help yourselves to the food and drink." With that, he moved away from them and Maudie to the edge of the crowd, joining Rome Hampstead, everyone's favorite barber, and octogenarian Stewie Franks.

Jillian's glance landed on her grandmother, who beckoned her.

"Excuse me a second," she said to Hunter, Savannah, and James.

"Is everything all right?" Bertie asked in a low voice when Jillian got to her.

"I hope so."

Maudie remained where she was, the puppies in her arms. Wanda Jean stood beside her, talking and gesturing. Maudie said nothing as she gazed across the lawn at her husband.

"I'll take her a nice cool lemonade," Lenora said, filling a glass. "She looks like she needs one."

"She'll have to set one of the pups down first," Bertie said.

"I know." Lenora gave her a smile as she moved away. "Poor me, I might just have to snuggle those adorable little things for a minute so she can enjoy some refreshment."

The evening wore on, layering warm humid air with increasing darkness. The circular solar lights shone like tiny eerie spaceships near the ground, and someone lit the paper lanterns, which glowed colorfully. Laughter and conversation flowed, and the band changed from 1960s rock music to more mellow tunes that blended into the atmosphere rather than invading it.

Farris and Della never seemed to lack for company, but Hugh kept his distance.

"I don't think Hugh has spoken to his brother since they shook hands," Jillian said to Hunter as they dug into their slices of Bertie's scrumptious coconut cake.

He followed her gaze to Hugh, who—after cutting the cake with Maudie in a reenactment of their wedding day—had returned to the company of Stewie and Rome. Stewie, a quick-witted widower with a knack for storytelling, was relating a yarn that had captured the other men's full attention, then all three burst into guffaws.

"His reaction wasn't exactly what Maudie had hoped for, I'm afraid," Hunter replied.

"Not at all." Jillian gazed toward Maudie, who hadn't let Trudy or Roscoe out of her sight. "At least he did seem pleased to see his cousins again." She glanced around the crowd. "I saw them talking with him earlier, but I think they've already left."

"Maudie is delighted with Hugh's gift to her," Savannah said as she and James joined them. "More so than all the other gifts on that table, including those two crystal goblets with the gold-leaf trim that Wanda Jean gave them."

"With Hugh and Maudie staying away from each other and neither one really mingling with their guests, everything seems out of whack tonight," Jillian said with a sigh. "The only situations that seem to be par for the course are Bertie, Aunt Cornelia, and Lenora making sure everyone is taken care of and Wanda Jean chattering to everybody like a magpie."

"I overheard Wanda Jean doing her best to wangle information from Hugh's sister-in-law a few minutes ago," James said.

"Oh, yeah? What kind of information?" Jillian asked.

"Why the two haven't seen each other for so long, why Farris and Della have never been to Moss Hollow, why no one even knew Hugh had a brother, how long they planned to stay. I don't remember everything she asked. The list was long."

"Bless her heart, Wanda Jean has never been the soul of tact," Jillian said.

"That's true," James agreed, "but I'm kind of curious about the whole situation. Aren't you?"

"Naturally," Jillian said. "But I figure it will all come out soon enough."

James sighed wistfully.

Savannah giggled at him, then leaned over and kissed him loudly on the cheek. "My nosy hubby."

"Not nosy," James said. "Curious."

"Oh, of course," Savannah teased.

The four of them laughed.

"I saw Wanda Jean earlier, grilling Sheldon and Starla," Hunter said.

"Maybe she got the lowdown from them, but I doubt it," James said. "They were none too friendly. I don't think they understand our Southern small-town ways."

The music stopped as the band members took a break to get something to eat and drink. The absence of their sound gave the party a slightly lopsided aura, as if something had been lost.

"Hello!" Jillian exclaimed as one of the puppies frolicked across the grass to her as if greeting a long-lost friend. "This is Trudy. We met earlier." She picked up the pink-collared pup, who licked the end of her nose.

"That is the cutest puppy I've ever seen." Cornelia approached, carrying a plate of food. She stopped next to Hunter and took a bite of her sandwich. "But I'm partial to cats, you know."

"We know," everyone chorused. No pet—past, present, or

future—would ever usurp Possum's place in Cornelia's heart.

"Where's Bertie?" Hunter asked.

"She's involved deep in a conversation with Laura Lee. They're talking about some silly something in a novel they both read, and I had no interest in it at all. Here, Hunter. Would you hold my supper while I cuddle this adorable creature for a minute?" Cornelia handed him her half-full plate without waiting for a reply.

They watched while she baby-talked the puppy in her arms, nuzzling the soft head and enduring pink-tongued licks.

"Don't hog that puppy, Cornelia," Lenora said as she joined them.

For a while, Jillian was hard-pressed to know which of the two women was the softer touch. Maudie came over with Roscoe in her arms, and all three women acted like new grandmas at a church nursery.

"Maybe you all need to get yourselves a dog," Jillian said to Lenora and her great-aunt.

They looked at her as if she'd recommended they learn to drive race cars.

"Why on earth would you suggest something you know perfectly well would get Possum in a snit?" Cornelia asked.

"I can't keep a dog in my apartment, and you know it," Lenora declared.

"Well, you both seem so enamored with Trudy, I just thought you might—"

"Stop thinking so much," Cornelia said sternly. "Hunter, may I have my plate? I've hardly had time to eat today." She glanced at Maudie. "Are you having a good time?"

Maudie's smile was a little sad. "It's been very nice. You ladies did a great job with the food. I've heard nothing but high praise about all of it."

"I'm glad. But honey, you seem rather down for a woman

celebrating fifty years with a loving husband," Cornelia pointed out. "This party has surely made me wish my Raymond was here to enjoy it with us, but Bertie didn't think I should bring a cat with us, no matter how special he is."

"I'm sorry to be so gloomy. I'm just disappointed that Hugh and his brother aren't having the reunion I envisioned for them," Maudie said. "It took me a while to track down Farris and his wife. I searched online, and for a time, I thought for sure I was going to have to hire that detective over in Bristow. But it all worked out eventually."

"Hugh does seem pretty standoffish with the man and his wife," James said.

Lenora nodded. "I reckon it's awkward after so many years."

"But it seems peculiar to me that they wouldn't be inseparable, trying to catch up on all the time they've been apart." Maudie heaved out another long breath.

"I'm sure that it's because of whatever estranged them in the first place," Jillian said. "Maudie, don't you know what caused their separation?"

She shook her head. "I never even knew about Farris until recently, and even then, Hugh refused to say anything more than he hadn't seen the man since the late '60s."

"It must have been something major," Cornelia said.

Maudie's face registered sadness and confusion. "I don't know. I just don't know."

"I'll tell all of you something," Cornelia said. "If Bertie and I were separated because of some kind of tiff or whatever, I'd do anything to fix it."

Jillian smiled tenderly at her beloved great-aunt. Cornelia and Bertie often bickered and picked at each other like two young girls, but never, in her wildest and most terrible imaginings, could she envision those two dear women divided and silent. She turned to gaze at Hugh, who seemed perfectly and happily oblivious to his relative's presence at the party that night.

"Maybe they'll start catching up tomorrow," Maudie said. "They're staying with us for a few days."

"So Hugh had no idea his brother was coming?" Savannah asked.

"Not in the least," Maudie said. "Maybe he's just so surprised that he doesn't know how to react. Once I located Farris and Della, and knew they would be able to be here, I was very careful to keep the news quiet. I never realized Hugh didn't like big surprises. They've never seemed to bother him before."

Jillian bit her lip to keep from blurting out that everyone in town had known there would be a mystery guest.

Cornelia had no such hesitation. "For goodness' sake, Maudie. You know nothing stays secret in Moss Hollow. Everyone knew you had a mystery guest coming."

"I told only one person, and I didn't mention it to her until day before yesterday." Maudie's gaze sought and found Wanda Jean, who was near the food table with Annalise Reed, talking behind her hand, watching the musicians as they regathered.

Jillian shifted uncomfortably as Maudie made the connection between her best friend and the spread of her secret.

"What's going on over there?" Maudie said a few seconds later. She frowned as she looked across the lawn toward the bandstand. "What're they doing?"

Della had linked her arms with Hugh and was more or less tugging him to the stage, talking and gesturing.

"Maybe he's finally thawing a little," Lenora said.

"But she's not his blood relative, like Farris," Maudie said without taking her eyes off the pair.

"More than likely she's trying to break the ice for him," Hunter said.

Maudie glanced at him. "You think so?"

"I bet that's exactly what she's doing," James said before Hunter could answer. "She seems like a friendly lady, and I'm sure she wants the two to act like brothers again just as much as you do."

Maudie turned to observe Hugh and Della again. "That would be nice. But why are they talking to the band?"

James followed her gaze. "When they first got here, she seemed to want to meet everyone, so she probably wants Hugh to introduce her to the band."

"I reckon that makes as much sense as anything else," she said.

James glanced at the others. "I'm going to get some lemonade. Can I bring anyone a fresh drink?"

"Yes, please," Savannah said, holding up her empty glass.

Jillian nodded. "Thank you."

"Maudie? Cornelia?"

"That would be nice, if you'd be so kind as to take it over there where Bertie is sitting," Cornelia said. "I'm going to join her and get off my feet."

Maudie shook her head. "None for me, thank you. Hugh set up a place for the puppies in the house, so I'm going to take them inside. I'll be back directly." For a little while, though, Maudie remained where she was, cuddling the now-sleeping puppies in her arms. She never took her eyes off her husband and his sister-in-law.

"C'mon, Hunter," James said. "You can carry some of the drinks." The two men ambled off toward the refreshments.

Jillian started to turn away, but Della's expression as she gazed at Hugh caught her attention. Even from the distance and despite the rather dim outdoor lighting, Jillian read something on the woman's face that made her uncomfortable. Her expression was too soft and too warm, and she stood too close to him. Was that what had caught Maudie's attention?

"Excuse me," Maudie said suddenly. "I'm going to put the pups to bed." Jillian watched as the woman headed toward the house. She walked quickly, glancing neither right nor left, speaking to no one as she left the yard.

"What is it?" Savannah asked Jillian. "Why are you frowning?"

"That." She tipped her head toward Hugh and Della.

Savannah studied the pair, then murmured, "Oh dear."

"What are you talking about?" Wanda Jean asked from behind them, startling them both. The woman's nosiness was usually a mild irritation and frequently a humorous distraction, but right then she seemed intrusive and completely lacking discretion.

A loud drumroll stopped all talk and drew everyone's attention to the band, saving Jillian the need to reply to Wanda Jean's query.

One of the musicians spoke into the microphone. "Hey, y'all. It's been a fun evening so far, and I promise you, it's about to get even better. But first of all, congratulations to our happy bride and groom of fifty years. What a milestone!" When the applause died down, he continued. "Hugh and Maudie are the stars of the show tonight, but do you realize we have celebrities in our midst?"

"We do? Who?" Wanda Jean stared hard at the band members, all middle-aged men from Bristow who were generally hired to play for parties. As far as Jillian knew, they weren't well-known outside of Nathan County.

"You haven't heard from these two in a while," the speaker continued. "In fact, I've just been told they haven't performed since 1968." He grinned. "But when they were together on stage—hoo boy!" He shook his hands as if they were on fire.

"Who *is* he talking about?" Wanda Jean asked again. She glared around at the crowd, apparently trying to find a famous face among them and failing to notice Hugh and Della stepping onto the bandstand.

Savannah gripped Jillian's arm. "Are you kidding me? Hugh Honeycutt, a singer?"

Based on the whispers and chuckles that rippled through the

crowd, the situation surprised everyone.

"Say what?" Wanda Jean practically shrieked as she spotted the pair onstage.

"Where's Maudie?" Jillian stood on her tiptoes and tried to spot their hostess. She saw Hunter and James returning, each carrying cups of icy lemonade.

"What do you think of this development?" Hunter asked as he reached her.

She took the cup he offered. "I don't know what to think, but from the looks of it, we're about to find out."

On the bandstand, the band members, Hugh, and Della stood in a tight circle with heads together, talking. The crowd stirred restlessly, anticipation crackling through the humid night. The cluster of people on stage finally broke apart, the musicians taking up the instruments, Della grinning, and Hugh wearing the same expression he might if he'd stepped in something rotten. The fellow who had acted as emcee handed a cordless microphone to him and another to Della, pointing out the features.

He briefly took back the one Hugh held, turned to the crowd and said, "Ladies and gentlemen, a round of applause for the Country Sweethearts and their reunion concert!"

The applause was loud and enthusiastic, accompanied by a few shouts and even a whistle or two. The drummer beat time with his sticks and both men with guitars played a few chords. Hugh tapped his foot and glanced at Della, who swayed slightly with the rhythm of the beat.

"I was just a boy from Tennessee," he sang.

She echoed the tune, singing, "And I was a lonely city girl."

At first their voices were rather quiet, as if they were testing their abilities. Then, as they gained confidence, the sound blended into perfect harmony and the volume increased. A few lines later, it was as though they had fit into a place that had been empty for far too long. The song, country in flavor and tone, was the love story of a mismatched pair who yearned for each other. They belted out the words, strong and sweet, moving on stage as if fifty years hadn't passed since they'd last performed together. It seemed that decades lifted from them, revealing the two hopeful singers they had once been.

If Jillian thought the polite applause earlier had been loud, it was nothing compared to the thundering ovation offered as the last word of the song died away. Hugh's face was beaded with sweat, and Della's round cheeks were rosy. They looked at each other as if stunned by what they'd just done, then Della threw out both arms, her rich laughter ringing out, and she embraced him.

"We still got it, darlin'!" she said into the microphone.

"Sing another," someone called from the crowd, but Hugh held up one hand and shook his head.

"I'm not twenty-one anymore," he replied.

"Well I am!" Della turned to the band. "We'll sing 'Jackson.' Can you play it?"

The band members nodded, and one of the guitarists played a lively intro.

"C'mon, Hugh honey, let's sing it like we used to." Della grinned at Hugh and grabbed his free hand.

By the time they finished the classic song made famous by Johnny Cash and June Carter, playing off of each other like a finely tuned team, Jillian was wondering why what seemed to her like a promising career had been cut short.

"I can hardly believe my ears." Savannah's eyes were wide as she stared toward the musicians. "James, did you know Hugh could sing like that?"

"Not the least notion."

"He's not even in the church choir," Hunter said.

"The way Maudie and Wanda Jean like to talk about everything,

I wonder why they've never mentioned it." Jillian's glance fell on Maudie, who stood apart from everyone else, arms folded across her front as if protecting herself from the cold. "Or maybe she didn't know."

"Surely she knew," Savannah said. "I mean, how could she not?"

"She didn't know about Farris," James reminded her.

"That's true. I wonder what else she didn't know." Savannah turned to look at Hugh and Della standing arm in arm and beaming at each other. Jillian followed her gaze, and an uneasy feeling began to form.

4

"You don't suppose—" Jillian began, staring across the lawn at Hugh and Della.

"I know what you're thinking, because I'm thinking the same thing and hating it," Savannah said.

James frowned. "Hugh Honeycutt is one of the best guys in Moss Hollow, and what's wriggling around in your minds is wrong."

"You're right." Savannah patted his arm. "We're not implying that he's anything less than a good man. But he was young once and very talented. I just wonder if . . . I mean, I'm sure he had girlfriends before Maudie."

"And you think Della was one of them?" James asked.

"Maybe not." Jillian forced a hopeful tone into her voice. "If nothing else, it's obvious they had a promising start in the music industry. It's quite likely they were simply good friends and singing partners, and what we're seeing now is a reunion of that friendship. Performing together tends to make people closer than just friends, but that doesn't mean it was romantic."

Once again, they turned toward the duo, who were now surrounded by partygoers. In spite of what she'd just said, Jillian wasn't convinced Hugh and Della had merely sung together years ago. From the expression on Maudie's face as she walked toward the group, she harbored her own uneasy suspicions.

Wanda Jean hurried across the lawn to her friend. She clasped Maudie's arm to halt her, and the two of them talked intently for a few moments.

The band resumed playing. This time, the tunes were country, especially the older songs that had been made popular by the likes of Patsy Cline and Hank Williams.

"Let's dance," Jillian said to Hunter, hoping that being in his arms while soft, slow music played would chase away speculations that plagued her thoughts.

He cocked his head, listening. "That's 'The Tennessee Waltz,' isn't it?"

"I believe so."

"Isn't that the one about a girl whose friend steals her sweetheart?"

Jillian nodded mutely. And as they swayed, she couldn't help but wonder if the song might be a little too fitting for Maudie.

The next afternoon, the Southern Sweetie Pies gathered at The Chocolate Shoppe for their traditional Sunday meeting. Laura Lee Zane, a deputy sheriff, first gave a demonstration for a quick and simple pastry she'd discovered on the Internet, then she passed around flaky bars filled with chocolate, pecans, and just a touch of dried cayenne pepper.

The others raved over the taste and texture and the unexpected kick of flavor. Laura Lee handed out recipe cards, including the website address where she'd discovered the treat. "I almost didn't bring these today," she said, "because I thought y'all might hate the taste of the pepper. But last night at the party, Bertie convinced me to at least give you the option of hating or liking them."

"They're tasty. Nearly as spicy as Maudie's life," Wanda Jean said, licking the ends of her fingers.

Maudie, who'd missed church that morning, sat next to her, clad in jeans and a T-shirt. Her snow-white hair had been neatly combed in its usual pixie style, but her pale face was bare of makeup. In a group of women, most of whom were still in their church clothes, she seemed uncomfortable, and maybe even a little ill. Jillian doubted Maudie's demeanor and appearance had anything to do with what she was or was not wearing.

Maudie gave her best friend a small frown and a shake of the head. Some of the other women didn't seem to notice her discomfort and peered at her with open curiosity.

"What happened last night after the party?" local librarian Josi Rosenschein asked.

Maudie met her gaze. "Everyone went home, and we cleaned up the mess."

Annalise Reed, a banker's wife, cleaned her fingers on a napkin. "What about Hugh and that woman?"

"Do you mean Della?" Maudie asked innocently. "What about them?"

"Did she and Hugh really used to sing together?" Annalise asked.

"I think there was more to Hugh and Della than singing together." Wanda Jean nearly smiled as she spoke.

Maudie shifted and looked miserable.

"That's enough of the third degree," Jillian said. "I think we'd all better put a lid on our curiosity."

"That's right." Savannah nodded in agreement. "We need to remember we're the Southern Sweetie Pies, not the staff of a cheesy tabloid. A person has a right to privacy, even in Moss Hollow."

"Even in a Sweetie Pie meeting," Bertie added. "In fact, we—"

"It's okay," Maudie said, straightening. "I might as well tell you. If I don't, the rumors will run through town like an outbreak of hives."

Jillian thought that Maudie's willingness to halt gossip before it could find root was admirable, but if anything was true in Moss Hollow, it was that stories often took on a life of their own no matter their humble beginnings.

"It's quite simple, really," Maudie said. "Hugh and Della met when they were in their early twenties and had plans to become singers. They wrote a few songs and recorded that one you heard last night. It got some play on a few local radio stations in Missouri and seemed like it might get some national airplay. Then Farris and Della ran off and got married all of a sudden. That was that. No more Country Sweethearts." She sat back. "There you have it."

A stunned silence fell.

"'That was that' and 'there you have it'?" Wanda Jean frowned at her. "That can't possibly be all there is to it, Maudie."

"Of course it is."

Wanda Jean folded her arms. "Hugh hasn't seen his brother in all these years just because Farris married that girl?" Maudie gave a quick nod. Wanda Jean stared hard at her. "Excuse me if I think you're holding something back."

"She's right," Annalise said. "You are leaving out a big part of this story."

Bertie stood up and faced the group. "There is no law that says Maudie has to tell the Southern Sweetie Pies, or even her best friend, everything that's ever happened in her life. She has a right to privacy, and we need to respect that. That goes for all of us."

"All I'm saying is—" Wanda Jean began.

Maudie jumped to her feet. "I told you enough, and if I get wind of any dirty gossip about me, I'm blaming all of you." She glared at Wanda Jean. "Especially you." She grabbed her purse and rushed out of the bakery.

Everyone sat in silence for a few moments, staring at Wanda Jean and one another.

"Did you ever?" Cornelia asked finally.

"I don't blame her." Lenora shifted in her chair. "We might not be on staff at some cheesy magazine like Savannah said, but we sure did act like it. I am ashamed of every single one of us."

"All we're doing is trying to be her friends." Wanda Jean sniffed. "She didn't have to get so huffy."

Bertie got to her feet. "I believe it's time to end this week's meeting. Laura Lee, thank you for sharing your tasty recipe. See you all back here next week, preferably with your minds on baking instead of gossiping."

"I'll tell you two something you probably already know," Cornelia said that night at the supper table.

"In that case, why bother wasting our time?" Bertie asked. "Jillian, honey, you did a good job with this chicken salad. I like it when you add grapes and water chestnuts. And the mandarin oranges give it zip."

"Thanks, Bertie. Next time, I might try—"

"Wanda Jean is right," Cornelia continued as if neither had spoken. "Maudie is not telling us everything."

"Now, Aunt Cornelia."

Cornelia shook her index finger at Jillian. "Don't you 'Aunt Cornelia' me. I've been around many a year, and I know when someone is hiding something. Maudie Honeycutt is hiding something, and we all know it."

"You're right, Sister, but we also know that it is none of our business." Bertie chewed on her lip a moment, then added, "Of course, I don't like seeing the poor woman upset. It's as plain as the nose on your face that she's troubled."

Cornelia set down her fork. "That's what I said."

Bertie started gathering and stacking their dirty plates. "No, you said she was hiding something."

"It's the same difference."

"How? Explain to me how it's the same."

The twins glowered at each other.

"If you don't know, I'm not going to explain it to you." Cornelia sniffed and looked away.

"That's the most foolish thing I've ever heard. A person who doesn't know something needs to have it explained to them. How do you think folks learn anything? The information just falls out of the sky?"

Jillian was in no frame of mind to listen to such nonsense. "I believe Aunt Cornelia means that Maudie would feel better if she wasn't hiding something from everyone."

"Exactly." Cornelia gave her an approving smile.

"No," Bertie said, "what my sister means is that *we'd* all feel better if we knew exactly what secret Maudie is keeping. But it's none of our business."

Cornelia stood, her smile gone. "Bertie, your negative energy is not encouraging. I'm going to go to my room to talk the situation over with Raymond. Good night."

"It's not even seven o'clock yet," Bertie said. "Hunter is coming over later. And so are Savannah and James. We're going to play Monopoly, remember?"

Cornelia grew thoughtful and tapped one finger against her cheek. "In that case, I might come back downstairs."

"But we are *not* going to discuss Maudie while they are here." Bertie's words were a command, not a request.

Once again, Cornelia took on the mantle of a martyr. "In that case, I'll just stay in my room. No one wants to listen to an old woman anyway." She left them, muttering to herself. Possum followed at her heels, his tail twitching.

Bertie watched them go and shook her head. "She's right, you know."

"That no one wants to listen to an old woman?" Jillian asked.
Bertie scowled. "No. That Maudie is keeping something back."
"Didn't you just say it was none of our business?"
Bertie flapped her hand dismissively. "I just said that so
Cornelia wouldn't get any harebrained ideas about taking her stack
of magazine inserts over for a séance at the Honeycutt house."
Jillian had to admit that was a possibility. She sighed. "Poor
Maudie. It's plain as day that whatever's bothering her is weighing
heavily."
"All through the meeting, it seemed like she was trying to
avoid attention. Did you notice?"
Jillian gave a snort. "She glared pretty hard at Wanda Jean."
"Sure, right before she left. But before we all started in on
her, she just sat there and stared at her hands."
Jillian propped her elbow on the table and rested her chin in
her hand. "You think she's sick, Bertie?"
"She's worried. That's what I think. That little concert last
night—it did something to her."
"It sure did," Jillian said. "She wasn't expecting something
like that, was she?"
"It didn't seem so. And the way that Della was so flirty with
Hugh." Bertie sipped her sweet tea, her eyes troubled. "Of course,
Hugh never flirted back. He didn't try too hard to get away from
her either, though."
Jillian took a drink of her own sweet tea. "Did you know
Hugh could sing like that?"
"I never knew Hugh could sing, period."
"Me either. As Hunter pointed out last night, he's not even
in the church choir. And once I got to thinking about it, I don't
believe I've ever seen or heard him sing in the congregation with
everyone else. Isn't that odd?"
"Given that strong voice he belted out, yes, it sure is. And

you're right. He never opens his mouth during the song service." Bertie hesitated a moment. "It seems to me that Maudie, of all people, would have known about how well he sings and would have mentioned it."

"I'm pretty sure she didn't know, Bertie. Crazy as it sounds, I think he kept it from her, just as he kept it from all of us. It's like he had a whole different life before Maudie, and he left it behind to the extreme that he didn't even tell her about it."

"I wonder why."

"We may never know." Jillian stood. "Let's get these dishes washed."

That night, after Hunter, James, and Savannah left Belle Haven and Bertie went to bed, Jillian sprawled on top of the covers in her coolest pajamas with a fan blowing across her warm skin. Cornelia had come down once as the others sat in the living room playing Monopoly. She greeted their guests, then stood behind Bertie and watched the game for a few minutes.

"Did you get any clarity, Aunt Cornelia?" Jillian had asked.

"Not yet. I came down to be polite, and now I'm going back to bed to continue my ponderings."

"You and me both," Jillian muttered as she stared up into the darkness of her bedroom. "If your ponderings aren't any better than mine, you're wasting brainpower."

As the soft hum of the fan's motor finally lulled her toward sleep, notions and images—both the possible and the outlandish— flitted through her mind like a kaleidoscope of butterflies. Jillian readily acknowledged that she was a ready and willing participant of delving into the pieces when she faced a puzzle. Nothing pleased her in quite the same way as sorting through and fitting those pieces together. She wanted to solve a mystery, no matter how simple or complex, no matter if it involved her or not. It was simply a part of what made her who she was, and trying to staunch that interest was as futile as spitting on a house fire to put it out.

"What is going on in the Honeycutt house?" she whispered to the night as she drifted into slumber.

The night did not respond.

Monday morning, Jillian was up to her elbows in hot, soapy water, scrubbing out the cinnamon roll pans, when Lenora bustled up to her, eyes big.

"You gotta see who's out there," Lenora said, sounding nearly breathless.

"Is Hunter here again? He already picked up—"

"No, not him. Here." Lenora offered a clean towel. "Dry your hands and go look. Just don't be goggle-eyed about it."

Mystified, Jillian did as she was told and slipped casually to the front area. Her gaze landed on a smiling Hugh Honeycutt at a small table. Across from him sat his sister-in-law, her thick, white-blonde braid shining in the morning sun. Her round cheeks were pink, and thick, false eyelashes framed her sparkling blue eyes. They each had coffee, wore big smiles, and chatted like old friends.

Jillian cast a glance around the bakery, seeking but not finding Maudie or Farris. From his usual table in the corner, Stewie Franks stared at Hugh and Della over the top of his newspaper. He met Jillian's eyes, raised one eyebrow, then lifted the paper higher, hiding himself from everyone else.

Della reached across the small space and took Hugh's hand. She leaned toward him, smiling and whispering as if she were sharing her deepest, darkest secret. The hair on the back of Jillian's neck prickled.

"The nerve," Lenora muttered next to her. "What are they thinking, coming here and acting like that? What's gotten into Hugh? Is Maudie here?"

Hugh pulled his hand free and moved back in his chair,

putting more distance between himself and his tablemate. If the simpering Della noticed, she gave no sign as she continued to talk with great intensity.

"I haven't seen her," Jillian whispered, "but I refuse to believe those two are anything more than two friends catching up on old times."

"He should be catching up on old times with his brother, if you ask me," Lenora said.

Bertie joined them, but apparently not to gape at Hugh and Della. She grabbed Jillian and Lenora by the elbow and led them away from the door. "Your gawking is indecorous, ladies," she said sharply.

"Not near as *indecorous* as it is for them to be sitting in public, holding hands," Lenora declared. "They didn't seem to mind us, and everyone else, gawking at them."

"They weren't really holding hands," Jillian said. "Hugh pulled away pretty quick."

"We know Hugh, and we know he would never do anything to hurt Maudie," Bertie said. "They've been respected citizens of this town forever, and it would be completely foolish for him to jeopardize their relationship and their reputation, especially at their age."

Lenora went to the worktable, where she began kneading some dough that she had left rising earlier. "There is no age limit to someone acting like a fool."

"That's true, but I flat-out refuse to believe the worst of Hugh Honeycutt." Bertie folded both arms across her chest and thrust out her chin.

"If it's all so aboveboard, then why isn't Farris or Maudie out there with them?" Lenora was clearly still skeptical. "Tell me that."

Bertie shrugged as she got back to her own work of frosting cupcakes. "Maybe they didn't want to come."

"This situation bears watching," Lenora said.

Bertie fixed an appraising gaze on Lenora. "You're sounding a lot like Wanda Jean."

Lenora's mouth flew open. "You take that back, Bertie Harper."

Jillian smiled. "If the shoe fits . . ."

"The shoe might fit, but I'm not wearing it," Lenora said. "And let me tell you—"

Lenora's rant was interrupted by Maggie poking her head into the kitchen. "Would one of you mind helping out here? We just got a bit of a rush."

"Jillian, you go," Bertie said, casting a sideways glance at Lenora. "Something tells me Lenora might be too distracted by some customers who've already been served to help the ones who haven't."

Jillian did as instructed. Soon enough, she and Maggie had the sudden rush of customers under control. Just as the line died down, the front door chimed again, and Wanda Jean and Maudie walked into the bakery. Jillian was glad to see they seemed to have made up after the scene at the Sweetie Pies meeting, but she cringed when Maudie spotted her husband and sister-in-law. Hadn't she known they were in the bakery?

Maudie paused only for the length of a breath, then sailed directly to Hugh and Della's table with Wanda Jean in her wake.

Hugh looked up and gave her a big smile. "Hi, honey."

"Fancy meeting you here," she said as she sat down next to him. Wanda Jean settled next to Della and said nothing as she very conspicuously moved her chair a couple of inches away from the woman.

"Didn't Farris want to come with you?" Della asked.

"He said he's going to check out the town first." Maudie met Jillian's gaze. "Do you have éclairs this morning?"

Jillian nodded. "We sure do. Would you like me to get you one, Maudie?"

"Bring each of us one, if you will, please," Hugh said.

"Not me," Della piped up. "I'm gluten intolerant. I'll just have coffee."

Jillian served the pastries and coffee, then returned to the kitchen. When she came back out to refill the case with bear claws a little while later, Wanda Jean was telling an old tale, and none too quietly.

"This was back in the '30s, mind you, but it happened just as I told you," she said, apparently nearing the end of her story. "So, as it turns out, old Homer Claussen got shot in the back by that angry husband, and Homer's widow was left with those thirteen kids to raise on her own. The man who shot him went to prison."

The pause was significant to anyone who knew Wanda Jean. She raised an eyebrow at Della, who merely blinked at her.

"How're the new pups?" Stewie called out, breaking into the awkward silence.

Hugh twisted in his chair to face Stewie. "They're fine."

"Fat as butterballs," Della added. "I've never seen such cute puppies."

"Too many dogs for my taste." Wanda Jean picked up her éclair, which she'd barely touched as she'd recounted her tale.

"I love all of them," Maudie said.

"I don't love the mess." Wanda Jean took an enthusiastic bite of her éclair. A huge blob of filling squished out and onto her plate.

Maudie drained her coffee and stood. "I need to get back to them."

"Already?" Wanda Jean asked. "I still have half of my éclair, and you haven't touched yours."

"Coming, Hugh?" Maudie's eyes never left her husband.

"I thought you were going to get groceries." He shot a look at Wanda Jean and another at Della.

"I'll get groceries later," Maudie said.

"I told Farris to meet us here," Della put in. "We should wait for him."

At these words, Hugh's face turned expressionless and he stood. "I'll take Maudie home, and you can wait here for him if you want." Without pausing for a response, he grabbed Maudie's hand and hustled her out the door.

Della stared after them, then scrambled to her feet. "Wait for me," she said as she rushed to catch up.

Left alone at the table, Wanda Jean gaped at Jillian. "Mercy! Did you see that? They just went off and stranded me."

"I saw. But you're hardly stranded." She pointed toward the parking lot. "Your car is right there."

Wanda Jean sniffed. "I know, but still. I don't understand why she'd just leave me without so much as a backward glance." She blinked hard and dropped her gaze.

Jillian grabbed the coffeepot from the warmer and carried it to her table. "How about a refill?"

"Thank you, honey." Wanda Jean cleared her throat. "Do you have a minute to talk to me, Jillian?"

"Sure. Just let me put the coffee back." Jillian filled a cup for herself, then she sat down across from Wanda Jean and waited.

The woman stared out at the parking lot a few seconds, then blew out a deep sigh and turned to her. "I'm worried sick."

"About Maudie?"

Wanda Jean nodded and swallowed hard. "About Maudie. About Maudie and Hugh. About me and Maudie." She gathered in another breath and let it out slowly. "I've never told this to anyone, but the truth is, I've always envied Hugh and Maudie."

"Really?" Jillian was surprised. Wanda Jean had been a widow for years, but she'd always made it fairly clear that being single suited her just fine.

Wanda Jean gave a small smile and lifted one shoulder.

"They have such an enviable life. They've always been so close, and they hardly ever bicker. I never had that kind of relationship. My husband was pretty stern, and he wasn't very kind to me or to anyone else. I'm happier as a widow, and that's the honest truth. But that doesn't mean that I haven't envied my best friend her happiness. I don't begrudge it, mind you. I just wish I'd been lucky enough to find some of my own." She paused and waited for Jillian to say something.

"I understand." Jillian took a sip of coffee. "I'd rather be single than tied to someone who treated me poorly, or who didn't love me."

"Maudie and Hugh have always had pretty much the perfect marriage, at least in my eyes."

"I've never heard a cross word between them, but no one has a perfect relationship, Wanda Jean. She was pretty upset when he was late for the party."

"I know." Wanda Jean toyed with her napkin. "Of course, him getting her those two puppies wiped out her vexation for a while. She loves dogs, let me tell you. If they lived where there wasn't a pet limit ordinance, their house would be overrun with every stray dog from here to Alabama."

Jillian chuckled. "That's for sure."

"Anyway, I don't know what the deal is about Hugh's brother and why Hugh treats him like a rank stranger, but there's something. And it's affecting my friend in a way I've never seen before."

Before agreeing outright, Jillian fleetingly thought about Wanda Jean's penchant for spreading gossip. Trying to be diplomatic, she said, "She has been acting a little different."

"Different is not the word for it, Jillian. And she absolutely refuses to talk to me. Maudie has never, ever not talked to me before." Wanda Jean used the napkin she'd been toying with to blot her eyes. "This situation is tearing my heart out in so many different directions that I just plain don't know what to do."

"Did you try to talk with her this morning?" Jillian asked.

"I did. When I asked her how things were going, she nearly took my head off. I'm telling you, Jillian, she has never been this way before, and it has something to do with those in-laws. More specifically, that woman Della."

"What did she tell you about Della and Farris before they showed up?"

As upset as she was, Wanda Jean wriggled in her seat and leaned forward in her favored gossiping posture. *There's the Wanda Jean I know.*

"She didn't know Hugh had a brother," Wanda Jean said. "I was the only one she told."

"Yes, you mentioned that the other day."

"Given how close they've always been, I don't understand how she could be married to him all these years and not know anything about Hugh's family. But as soon as she found out about Farris, she decided to invite him for a visit. When she told me that she planned to invite him as a surprise for Hugh, I tried to talk her out of it. I said, 'Maudie, there is something weird about this whole situation.' In fact, I told her she'd better not be bringing in someone Hugh hadn't spoken to or even spoken of in the whole time they'd been together. And you know what she said?"

"I bet you'll tell me."

"She said, 'If they have hard feelings for each other, then it's high time to close the book on that chapter and open the page to forgiveness.'" Wanda Jean's voice broke and she stopped, looking away again as if embarrassed to be caught tearful. "That's just like Maudie. She cares so much. She can't stand the idea of a broken relationship."

"Nobody would disagree with that," Jillian said.

Wanda Jean's eyes brimmed with worry and pleading. "How

do I help my friend when she doesn't want it?"

Jillian reached out and gave her hand a gentle squeeze. "Maybe she does want it, Wanda Jean, but she can't figure out how to let you know. Maybe she's so overwhelmed and confused right now, she doesn't know which way to turn."

"Could be she wants to be left alone so she can think." Lenora had materialized beside their table without Jillian noticing. "You gotta understand that everyone handles situations differently."

Wanda Jean sighed. "For years, anytime either of us has a problem or concern, we talk to each other about it. And Hugh too. I can't tell you how often he and Maudie have helped me through rough patches. And now, it's time for me to help, and I—" She stopped abruptly and gazed down at her lap. "I feel like I'm failing my two best friends."

"You can't see it that way. She's just not ready for your help," Lenora said. "You've let her know you're around when she needs you. She'll come to you when she feels the time is right."

Wanda Jean regarded her impassively. "Maybe. But I'm telling you both, there is something fishy about those people. So fishy they practically stink."

"And here's a chance for the rest of us to see how badly they stink," Jillian murmured. "Farris is coming in."

Farris Honeycutt looked a lot like his brother, but thinner, with a bit less hair and a more weathered face. He stopped just inside the door and scanned the area, then approached Maggie at the counter. "Excuse me. I'm trying to find my wife. I thought she said she'd be here."

Wanda Jean sniffed hard, wiped her eyes, and straightened her shoulders. She turned toward Farris and called, "You're Della's husband, aren't you?"

He gave her a startled glance, then nodded as he walked over with a tentative smile. "You know Della?"

"Not really, but I know Maudie. And I know your brother."

"Oh yeah?"

Wanda Jean did not return his smile. Instead, she laced her words with as much meaning as she could. "Maudie and I have known each other all our lives. We're best friends. And Hugh is like a brother to me. I love those people dearly."

"That's great. I'm glad you are so close." Farris passed another glance around the bakery as if he might have overlooked his wife. "Do you know where they are? I thought they were coming to The Chocolate Shoppe."

"They were here," Wanda Jean said, "but they left a few minutes ago."

"Do you know where they went?" Farris asked.

"Not a clue." Wanda Jean fixed an assessing gaze on him. "Why didn't you come with them instead of running around town on your own?"

A slight frown embedded itself on his forehead as he took his cell phone out of his shirt pocket. "I beg your pardon?"

"If you had come with Hugh and your wife, you wouldn't be searching for them now." Wanda Jean's clipped words were full of accusation.

"I always take a walk in the morning. Good for the heart, my doctor says. They said they'd meet me here." Farris tapped the screen, then held the phone to his ear, glancing around once more. Annoyance crossed his features, deepening his frown. "I don't know why I bother to call her. She never answers." He turned off the phone and returned it to his pocket.

"I'll call Maudie." Wanda Jean dug around in her purse.

"They left about fifteen minutes ago," Jillian said. "Best guess is that they're heading back to the house."

Farris nodded. "Okay. I'll go back there. Thank you." He dipped his head toward Wanda Jean as she pulled her phone from the depths of her purse. "Don't bother calling, ma'am. Thank you anyway."

The women watched as he left.

Wanda Jean slumped in her chair. "I believe I could have handled that better."

Staring after Farris, Jillian wasn't sure about that. Was it just her imagination, or was there something strange about Hugh's brother?

Thursday morning, while Bertie washed a large stainless steel mixing bowl, she said, "I reckon Hugh's brother and his wife are leaving today."

"Where'd you hear that?" Lenora asked as she slid two large pans of lemon bars into the oven.

"Someone mentioned it yesterday afternoon while you were at the dentist," Bertie said.

Jillian glanced up from putting the finishing touches on Holly Harkin's birthday cake. "I wonder how Maudie's doing by now."

"I imagine we all wonder that, with her not coming in here since Monday," Lenora said. "And Wanda Jean hasn't been here either. You know, I felt downright sorry for her the other day. She seemed so misplaced without Maudie."

"In all these years, I've never known Wanda Jean to act lost." Bertie finished drying her bowl and brought it back to the worktable to start another batch of muffins. "She's always been independent. And hardheaded. I'll tell you the honest truth, I hope those Honeycutt in-laws go back to wherever they came from and things get back to normal, even if that means Maudie and Wanda Jean set up in here and gossip about everything under the shining sun again." She peeked over at the pink rosettes Jillian had piped on the birthday cake and smiled. "You've become a good cake decorator."

"One of the best I've seen," Lenora added.

Jillian blushed at their praise. The two baking veterans were hard to impress. "Coming from the two best bakers in town, I take that as a compliment."

Bertie started to turn her attention back to her muffins, but then she looked back at Jillian's cake. A small frown crinkled her forehead.

"Something wrong?" Jillian asked as she laid down the pastry bag. She studied her work, searching for defects but seeing none.

"You said you were making that for Holly Harkin's birthday?" Bertie asked.

"That's right."

"Her birthday is in October. Why are we making her cake in July?"

"Eddie says she finds out about everything he plans, every year, so this year, he's going to fool her by having her birthday party this weekend."

The women laughed, and Lenora shook her head. "Now that's a good trick." She paused, then added, "He's not dragging in some long-lost relative to add to the surprise, is he?"

"I surely hope not, for Holly's sake," Jillian said. "And Eddie's."

Late that afternoon, Jillian had just sold the last of that day's bear claws and was carrying the empty tray to the sink for washing when the phone rang.

"Honey, you or Bertie best come home, if one of you can get away." There was no mistaking the anxiety in Cornelia's voice.

A shiver skittered down Jillian's spine. "What's wrong?"

"Maudie's here," Cornelia whispered, "and I don't know what to do or say."

"Why? What's happened?"

"Just come *home*."

Jillian didn't like the fear she heard in her great-aunt's voice. "Sure, okay. I'll be right there."

Preferring not to disturb or worry her grandmother, Jillian said nothing about what may or may not be occurring at Belle Haven as she made a hazy excuse for leaving the bakery an hour early. On the way home, her active mind concocted all kinds of scenarios for Cornelia being upset by Maudie's presence at Belle Haven, but most of them were pretty outrageous and more than a little unlikely, even though you never really knew with Cornelia. Nevertheless, she drove at the rim edge of the speed limit and rushed inside the moment she'd parked the car.

She was immediately met by a flurry of clicking toenails, wagging tails, flying fur, and slobbery, panting breaths. Her first instinct against the onslaught was to take a giant step backward as two dogs and a puppy rushed toward her, barking excitedly. But then Jillian relaxed as she recognized her greeters: Maudie's two flop-eared basset hounds, Mosey and Ambler, and one of the goldendoodle pups.

Cornelia hurried into the foyer, Maudie at her heels. With one piercing whistle, Maudie silenced the dogs. Both bassets immediately stopped barking and plopped onto their haunches, regarding Jillian with friendly brown eyes. The puppy tumbled to a stop beside them, tail whipping back and forth. Possum was nowhere in sight, and Jillian figured he had taken shelter upstairs under Cornelia's bed.

"What a welcome." Jillian bent to pet each dog in turn. Her attention was well received, earning her nuzzles and licks in return. "Hi, guys."

"They know you, Jillian," Maudie said with a wan smile. She looked as if she had neither eaten nor slept in a few days. "Okay, doggies, go lie down." She snapped her finger and pointed toward the sitting room. The hounds got up and trotted away, the pup following.

Cornelia met Jillian's eyes. "Honey, will you sit with Maudie while I go fix some tea?"

"Sure." Jillian turned to Maudie and tried to keep her tone light. "Let's join the dogs, shall we?"

Maudie nodded and let herself be guided back into the room where her pets had piled onto two dog beds. The puppy went to sleep immediately, snuggled up to Ambler, but Mosey watched the humans as if waiting to be summoned.

Jillian noted a basket bulging with yarn and bristling with crochet hooks near the fireplace. Next to it sat two large suitcases.

Maudie blew out a long breath as she sank into a chair. Her body seemed to shrink as she exhaled, which alarmed Jillian.

"Maudie, is everything all right?" Jillian asked as she took a seat nearby.

After another prolonged sigh, Maudie answered quietly, "No."

"Are you ill?"

Maudie cast a sideways look at her. "Only at heart."

"What's happened?" Jillian choked out the question despite being quite uneasy about what the answer might be. "Where's the other puppy?"

Maudie sniffled, then dug a tissue out of her pocket and dabbed at her eyes. She tried to speak, failed, and cleared her throat. "Roscoe isn't here," she finally croaked out.

"Did something happen to him?"

Maudie shook her head.

"Is he all right?"

"I think so."

"Maudie, you're being awfully cryptic. Please tell me what's going on."

"I can't."

"Can't? Why not?"

Maudie shook her head again. Getting information from her might prove to be a challenge.

"I see suitcases. Are you taking a trip?"

"No." Maudie picked up the sleeping Trudy and cuddled her close. For a little while, she silently stroked the puppy's golden head. Jillian knew the woman's sight was turned inward. She could have been stroking a porcupine and not realized it.

Cornelia brought in a tray with three cups of steaming tea and murmured, "Maudie is going to be staying here at Belle Haven."

Considering the suitcases and the dogs, this announcement didn't surprise Jillian. Although she strongly suspected the reason behind Maudie's visit, she wondered how long the woman truly intended to stay. *And what does Hugh think of this?* Surely he'd be coming soon to get his family and take them home. Maybe he was giving Maudie a little breathing space first.

"She'll stay in the room at the top of the stairs for now, but she's wondering about the butler's quarters. Here, honey." Cornelia handed Maudie a cup. "Chamomile sweetened with honey. It will relax you."

Jillian lifted her eyebrows. Those compact butler quarters on the second floor comprised a small kitchen, living room, bedroom, and bath, and they hadn't been used in a long time. Surely Maudie wasn't seriously considering moving in there.

"Will you, Jillian?" Cornelia's voice brought Jillian out of her thoughts.

"Will I what?"

"Get supper started while I help settle Maudie into her room?"

"Yes, of course." Jillian issued a quick, distracted smile and went to the kitchen. As she retrieved dinner fixings from the refrigerator, her mind whirred with wonder about Maudie's arrival at Belle Haven, what Hugh might have to say about it, and why the second goldendoodle hadn't come along with the other dogs.

She was snipping the stems off some fresh-picked green beans when Cornelia joined her. "Did you get Maudie settled?" Jillian asked.

Cornelia nodded. "I persuaded her to lie down until supper's ready. She says she hasn't slept but a few hours all week, and now this." She took the lid off a slow cooker and peered at the roast inside.

"And now what?"

Cornelia replaced the lid and looked at Jillian. "Why, whatever it is that has brought her to us. I'm sorry I called you away from the bakery, but for a minute, I was sure she was about to have a spell or something."

"Do you think Dr. Taylor would have been a better call to make?"

Cornelia waved off the idea. "Not the kind of spell a doctor could help with. That is, she doesn't seem to be sick or anything. But I'm afraid she's headed for a breakdown, and if so, that's when we'll have to call the doctor."

Jillian frowned, dried her hands, and turned to Cornelia. "What's going on?"

"That's just the thing. I wish I knew, but she won't talk."

"Do you at least know why she's here at Belle Haven instead of with Wanda Jean?"

"No, honey, I sure don't. She showed up at the door with her suitcases and her dogs, and she asked if they could all stay awhile. I'm not going turn anyone out, especially an old friend."

"But didn't you ask her what's going on?"

Cornelia pinned a reproving gaze on her. "Do you think I just fell off the turnip truck? Of course I asked. And she wouldn't tell me." She slid a head of cabbage across the counter to Jillian. "If you're done snipping those beans, shred this for coleslaw. I'll whip up some corn muffins."

"How can you think about food when we don't know what's going on with Maudie?"

Cornelia spread her arms, hands open, palms up. "What do you expect me to do, Jillian? Wring my hands and stare out the window?"

"No, but it seems odd to me that she turns up here with her suitcases and her dogs, and you didn't—"

"Didn't what? Force her at gunpoint to tell me what's wrong?" Cornelia shook her head. "She's a friend. She's showed up at our door, obviously hurt and needing a place to stay. There is no way on God's green earth I'm going to turn her away."

"That's not what I mean." There were few things in life that Jillian disliked more than being scolded by her grandmother, and one of them was being scolded by her great-aunt.

"Then what *do* you mean?" Cornelia's usually sweet face was fixed with a flinty expression.

Jillian ran the cabbage down the grater. "I'm worried about Maudie, and I'm sure you are too. She hasn't been herself since that anniversary party. She hasn't even come to the bakery since Monday, and you know that gossip and pastries with Wanda Jean was part of her daily routine. Speaking of whom, Maudie came here instead of going to her best friend."

Cornelia's face softened. "I know. Something's happened, but she obviously needs time to work things out in her mind before she talks. Let's give her that time without trying to pry information out of her. If and when she wants us to know what's happening, she'll tell us." She glanced toward the kitchen door and sighed. "And you know Maudie. She'll talk, eventually."

"I wonder if Wanda Jean at least knows what's going on."

Cornelia's glower returned, and she shook her index finger at Jillian. "Don't you go digging around in Maudie's personal life with that woman. Wanda Jean Maplewood might be her best friend, but she doesn't have enough to keep her busy. She goes hunting for gossip like it's an eight-point buck. That's been her trouble all these years."

"You have a point, Aunt Cornelia, but if Maudie is going to be sharing our home with us, shouldn't we be apprised of potential trouble?"

Cornelia wrinkled her nose. "Apprised of potential trouble? Jillian, you have been watching too many lawyer shows on television."

Jillian suppressed her annoyance. "All I'm asking is how can we help her if we don't know what she needs help with?"

"Have you not been listening to me?" Cornelia reached out and gently tugged one of Jillian's ears as if trying to make it work. "We can feed her, give her a safe and comfortable place to sleep, and we can assure her of our friendship. That is helping. We can only help her as far as she'll let us. Prying into her pain before she's ready to talk about it is the opposite of helpful. So you finish making that slaw and let me get on with my corn muffins."

If Cornelia, one of the most intrusive women in Moss Hollow, was advising personal space, that must be the right thing. Jillian wiped her hands on a towel. "I'll finish the slaw after I call Bertie. She shouldn't walk into a surprise like this."

"Do what you think is best, but tell her not to spread it around that Maudie's here. She wants it kept quiet."

"Bertie doesn't spread rumors," Jillian said as she picked up the phone and started to dial the bakery. "She just collects them."

Jillian, Bertie, and Cornelia waited an hour past their usual suppertime before Maudie showed herself again.

"Should one of us go and get her?" Jillian asked.

"Now, Jillian, you stop fussing. She'll come down when she's good and ready." For once, Bertie was fully on Cornelia's side, which meant arguing was simply a waste of breath. "If she's gotten as little sleep as my sister has said, I wouldn't wake her up for the world. We can just reheat the food when she's ready for it."

When Maudie finally came downstairs and into the living room where the Belle Haven women sat together, her pale-blue slacks and white blouse were rumpled, and her short hair stuck up in untamed spikes. All three dogs trailed her. She said nothing to her hosts or her dogs but walked straight through the room to the veranda doors and opened one. Mosey, Ambler, and Trudy scampered outside, and she followed.

Jillian watched through the veranda windows as Maudie roamed the backyard with her dogs. The canines snuffled the ground and every bush, shrub, tree, and flower that grew, but Maudie seemed indifferent to the world, even to Trudy's excited antics.

"I do hope they don't bring too much of the backyard in with them," Cornelia muttered.

"Hush. The floor is cleanable. Where's the cat?" Bertie asked.

"Possum has taken up residence in my room for the time being," Cornelia answered. "He does not seem to find that puppy as charming as the rest of us do."

"I wonder what happened to the other puppy," Jillian said.

"Apparently it's okay." Cornelia shrugged. "She indicated it was, anyway."

When Maudie came inside several minutes later, the dogs gazed at her expectantly and she extracted some dog biscuits from her pocket. She doled them out, one a time, but not before each recipient sat. Even Trudy sat for a few seconds. She lavished praise on each one, then pointed toward a ratty blanket that had replaced their beds near the fireplace.

"Go lie down." All of them obeyed her. Maudie smiled wanly

and turned toward her hostesses. "The baby will learn quickly, watching the adults."

"Now that they've had their snack, it's time to get the rest of us fed," Cornelia said. "Supper's in the warming oven, and the table's all set. Let's eat."

Jillian jumped up. "Yes, let's do. I'm starved."

"Y'all go ahead without me," Maudie said. "I don't have any appetite."

"Maudie, you have to eat or you'll get sick," Bertie said.

"You look peaked," Cornelia added.

"Really, I'm not hungry. Not a whit."

Bertie studied her pale face a moment. "When was your last meal?"

Maudie frowned, then her expression cleared. "It doesn't matter."

"When, Maudie?" Bertie's voice had taken on an edge of scolding.

"I guess it would be that plate of food you brought to me at the party, Cornelia. It was enough to feed a small army. And that slice of your delicious coconut cake, Bertie."

Jillian frowned. "Do you mean to say you haven't had a meal since Saturday night?"

Maudie shrugged. "I guess so. I've nibbled a bit here and there. I had to cook for our *guests*." She said the final word with such bitterness that the other three women exchanged glances.

"You come in the kitchen and eat something." Jillian took her arm.

"Oh, but—"

"Come on," Jillian said. Employing a certain tone she'd picked up from Bertie, she added, "Cornelia made a good supper for you, and I know you don't want to disappoint her by not eating it."

The tactic worked, and Maudie went along with them into

the kitchen, where Cornelia and Jillian quickly set the food out.

After Bertie said grace, Maudie passed an appreciative gaze over the food and said, "Everything looks and smells really good."

"And it'll do you good." Bertie picked up the bread basket. "Here, have a corn muffin."

About halfway through the meal, Cornelia asked with a bright, conversational tone, "Did your cousins from Nevada enjoy their visit?"

Maudie seemed to be confused by the question. "Who?"

"Your cousins from Nevada," Bertie said. "Starla, was it? And her husband."

"Oh, them." Maudie twirled her fork aimlessly in a pile of coleslaw. "They're from Arizona, not Nevada. They aren't big on little celebrations in rural areas. Both are firmly citified." She gave a weak little smile and ate a bite of slaw. "They left for Atlanta Sunday morning, and I suppose by now they're home. Or maybe they went to Dallas. Starla mentioned that they might."

"If they don't usually attend what you call 'little celebrations,' then it was nice of them to come to your anniversary party," Cornelia said. "Which, by the way, I would not call a 'little' celebration. It was well attended, and quite festive and fun."

"Starla and Sheldon already had the trip to Atlanta planned," Maudie explained with a shrug, "so our party was more or less coincidental. They wouldn't have come otherwise, I'm sure."

Cornelia's forehead furrowed. "That's too bad. Families should spend more time together. Why, look at us. Bertie, Jillian, and me, we're together all the time. Except when Jillian goes out with Hunter, of course. We don't go on their dates with them."

"For heaven's sake, Sister," Bertie scolded. "You say the silliest things."

"I don't see what's so silly about families being together a lot." Cornelia gave a haughty sniff.

By the end of supper, Maudie had eaten everything on her plate plus three corn muffins, and she no longer seemed quite as drawn and pale as she had when she'd come downstairs earlier.

"How about dessert?" Cornelia asked, getting up.

Maudie shook her head. "I'm full to the gills, thank you. Supper was just as delicious as everything you ladies make." Her smile was more like the sunny one she typically wore.

"Tonight we're having brownie trifle, with my homemade hot caramel sauce for it," Cornelia coaxed in a lilting singsong.

"Brownie trifle? That's Hugh's favorite." Maudie slumped in her chair, then stared out the window at nothing for so long that Jillian grew concerned.

"Are you okay?" Jillian asked gently.

"Hugh." Maudie said his name as if testing to see if she could pronounce it. "He's gone. That man has up and left me."

Jillian was sure she'd heard incorrectly. "I'm sorry, what?"

Maudie straightened in her seat. "Hugh has run off and left me high and dry."

"I don't believe it." Cornelia thrust out her chin and folded her arms across her chest as if a show of stubbornness would change Maudie's words.

"Whether you believe it or not, it's the truth." Maudie released an indignant breath before continuing. "When I got up this morning, he wasn't in bed or anywhere in the house. And what's more, he took Roscoe with him."

"That doesn't mean he left you," Bertie said. "Maybe the puppy was sick, and he took him to the vet."

Maudie narrowed her eyes. "If Roscoe had been sick, Hugh would have told me. Anyway, that's not the half of it."

"Then what is?" Bertie asked.

Maudie gathered a deep breath and met her gaze. "Seems that perky little sister-in-law of his has disappeared too."

"*What?*" Jillian, Bertie, and Cornelia squawked in unison like a trio of startled chickens.

Maudie said nothing.

"But weren't they leaving today?" Jillian asked.

"Farris is still here in Moss Hollow." Maudie's formerly pale face was starting to turn red. "In fact, he's still at the house!"

Cornelia raised her eyebrows. "At your house?"

Maudie nodded. "He has the cockamamy notion that Hugh is just showing Della the countryside. Said he'd wait there at the house because they were bound to come back."

"And they've both been gone since this morning?" Bertie asked.

"Or earlier," Maudie answered. "They were gone when I got up, so I have no idea what time they left."

"Maybe Farris knows where they went," Bertie suggested.

"He said he woke up before daylight, and Della wasn't there."

Jillian frowned. "Really? Did he get up and check to see if she was around somewhere?"

Maudie shrugged. "I don't think so. He said she often gets up early and goes for a walk or a drive. Sometimes even in the middle of the night. He said she's restless all the time."

"Does she leave him notes when she goes out?" Cornelia asked. "Did she leave him one this time? Did Hugh leave you a note? Did you check your answering machine? What about voice mail? Do y'all send text messages? Is any of his stuff missing? Did you call the sheriff?"

"For goodness' sake, Sister, take a breath." Bertie scowled at Cornelia, who glared right back.

Jillian cleared her throat loudly. "Has Hugh ever gone off like this before?"

"You mean without letting me know?" Maudie let out what could almost be considered a laugh. "Never. Not even to the grocery store or the gas station. Hugh's a thoughtful, kind man, and he always . . ." Her voice broke again. "It's that awful woman. She practically threw herself at him from the moment she saw him. You all saw her at the party."

"But Maudie—" Jillian began.

"They've run off together, I'm telling you," Maudie continued. "They've probably eloped. And taken my puppy with them, no less." She looked at Cornelia. "And no, I did not call the sheriff. It's none of his business. Nor Wanda Jean Maplewood's either. I've avoided her all week because she doesn't need to know all this. She'd have it all over town."

"Oh dear," Bertie said.

"But you have tried to call Hugh, right?" Jillian asked.

"Oh, I called this morning, but he didn't answer. He didn't call me back or text me or anything. So at this point, I am not calling that man again. If he was callous enough to leave me—and after fifty years, no less—I do not want to chase after him." She sniffed hard and clamped her jaw.

"But if he—"

"I'm not calling him, Jillian."

"Give me his phone number then, and I'll call him."

"No you won't!"

"Then I'll call Della. Maybe she—"

"I don't have her phone number, and even if I did, I wouldn't give it to you. Nor would I call her. And I'm through talking about this."

The Belle Haven women exchanged glances. Jillian was completely bewildered and knew her grandmother and great-aunt felt the same way.

Bertie reached for one of Maudie's hands. "Maudie, listen to me. You know married people can't elope with someone else. It's against the law."

Maudie nodded meekly. "I know."

"Try not to let your imagination run away with you," Bertie said. "You need to calm down and get a good night's sleep. Rest will help you tremendously."

"I don't see how rest is going to change anything," Maudie said huffily. "Will sleep bring my husband back to me? I don't think so, unless you're counting on him showing up in my dreams. Or nightmares."

"Let me fix you some chamomile tea," Jillian said. "That'll help."

"Or warm milk, if you'd prefer," Cornelia offered.

"I'm telling y'all, I doubt that I can get one wink of sleep,"

Maudie protested.

"Sure you can," Bertie said. "You have a nice quiet room upstairs. You've had a good supper, and you're surrounded by friends. We'll face this situation tomorrow when we're refreshed. Okay?"

Maudie nodded, and suddenly Jillian noticed the dark circles under her eyes. She was willing to wager the woman hadn't had a decent night's sleep since the previous Saturday.

"I'll even take care of the dogs for you," Jillian added.

"No, thank you," Maudie said. "I'll take care of them myself. They're like my kids, and they make me feel better." She sighed and looked in the direction of the sitting room. "Without my babies, I think I'd fall apart."

"I know what you mean," Cornelia said. "Possum is such good company when I'm here alone. He's always just right there, talking to me. Sometimes we sing."

For the first time, something other than despair showed on Maudie's face. "Sing? Possum sings?"

"No, Raymond sings, but Possum hums along."

"Oh good gravy," Bertie muttered. "Cornelia, some notions of yours are better left unexpressed."

But Cornelia continued as if she hadn't heard her sister. "Yesterday we made up a whole new verse for 'When the Roll Is Called Up Yonder.' You want me to sing it for you?" She sat up straight and cleared her throat.

"No, I do not. Nor do the rest of us." Bertie turned to Maudie. "Rest tonight. Tomorrow is a new day."

Cornelia smiled conspiratorially at Maudie. "Should we be naughty and eat our trifle in front of the TV? We have a nice selection of old movies. I see you brought your craft basket. You can show us what you're working on."

"Maybe tomorrow, thank you." Maudie's confession about

Hugh and the ensuing conversation seemed to have sapped whatever energy she'd had left. She got to her feet and made her way toward the stairs. "Supper was delicious, and I appreciate it, but if you'll excuse me, I'll go back to my room now."

Bertie cleared her throat. "Jillian, why don't you go with Maudie and make sure Cornelia gave her one of the good towels to use?"

"Why I—" Cornelia started, but Bertie sent her sister a silencing glare.

Understanding perfectly clearly that Bertie thought Maudie, in her fragile state, might need some help getting up the stairs, Jillian stood and followed their guest toward the steps. "Of course."

Maudie nodded in approval. "I might need to lean on you going up those steps, dear. I'm suddenly awfully tired."

Jillian smiled. "That's what a belly full of good food will do."

A whistle from Maudie got the attention of the dogs, and they made quite a parade ascending the staircase en masse. At the door of the guest room, Jillian bid Maudie and the dogs good night.

"If you need anything overnight, I'm just next door," Jillian said.

"Thank you." Maudie gave a small smile, but it quickly disappeared. "And whatever you do, do not call that man."

"But—"

"I mean it, Jillian. Give me your word."

"All right, if that's what you want."

"It is." Maudie started to slip into her room but leveled a hard look at Jillian. "And do not call anyone else. Not Wanda Jean, not Farris, not the sheriff. There is no reason to have him prowling around, asking embarrassing questions."

"All right, Maudie. I promise. Don't worry about anything right now. Just get some rest."

Back downstairs, Jillian settled on the living room sofa, legs crossed under her. Cornelia brought in a tray loaded with three helpings of brownie trifle topped with decadent hot caramel that

Jillian could smell all the way across the room.

Cornelia handed out the glass dessert dishes and took a seat next to Jillian. Jillian took a bite of trifle and nearly fell over with delight. *If anything can make me forget about the drama around here, it's chocolate and caramel.*

The three women ate without speaking for a while, and then Cornelia finally broke the silence. "Okay, girls, we have to do something."

"We *are* doing something," Bertie said. "We've taken her in, and we're watching over her."

"What did you have in mind, Aunt Cornelia?" Jillian set her dessert dish on the tray, more than a little sorry it was now empty.

"We should call Coy Henderson."

"For what reason?" Bertie asked.

"I declare, Bertie Alfreda. Haven't you been listening? Because Hugh is gone, and Coy needs to know."

"Now, Cornelia, you heard Maudie say she doesn't want the law involved," Bertie said.

Cornelia's spine straightened. "But I think we should anyway. What if it was Raymond who was missing? I'd be out driving up and down every road from here to St. Simons. Why, Hugh might be lying in a ditch, injured. Or worse."

Bertie glanced at Jillian. "What do you think, Jillian?"

"To be honest, the thought that he's hurt somewhere crossed my mind," Jillian admitted. "Hugh has always been so dependable and decent. It's hard to believe he'd just up and leave without a word or without getting in touch by this time. But Maudie doesn't want Coy involved, and she made me promise not to call him or Hugh."

"You didn't agree to such nonsense, did you?" Cornelia scowled.

"I did." Jillian shrugged helplessly. "Maudie doesn't want the law involved. And Hugh has only been gone since this morning, or thereabouts. For all we know, he might have gone to Atlanta to get Maudie another exotic dog or something."

Bertie heaved a long sigh. "Maybe. Let's hope it's nothing more serious than that. We don't always know about people. Everyone has a secret or two, and Hugh Honeycutt is no exception."

"He kept those two doodle dogs a secret," Cornelia pointed out, "so maybe that's what he did. Went somewhere to get more."

"I don't know what to think," Bertie said, "but I strongly doubt he's run off with that woman. And if you want to know the honest truth, I don't think he's in Atlanta buying a dog. I think we should at least call the hospitals."

"All right," Jillian said. "That's reasonable."

"And call Savannah." Cornelia wriggled her index finger at the phone in Jillian's hand. "And Lenora. And Hunter."

"Not on your life," Jillian said. "Maudie has made it crystal clear that she wants this whole situation kept quiet."

Cornelia sat back and huffed, staring at Jillian as if she'd never seen her before. "I can hardly believe you think your best friend, our good friend, and your beau would gossip."

Jillian felt a defensive tug. "I never said they would."

"You just as good as said it," Cornelia said.

Jillian shook her head. "If that's what you think, then you've misunderstood me. We've agreed to keep this situation under wraps as much as possible, so the fewer people who are chatting about it—with us or anyone else—the less chance for her personal life to become the biggest piece of grain in the town gossip mill."

"Jillian's right," Bertie said. "Folks don't mean to spread lies and rumors, but it happens when tongues start to wag."

Cornelia lifted both hands in surrender. "Okay, all right. If you both think that's best." She pinned her blue-eyed scrutiny on Jillian. "Of course you will call the hospital, won't you?"

"I said I would." Jillian brought up the number for the Nathan

County Hospital on her phone. "I'm curious how much Wanda Jean knows." She hadn't meant to speak this thought aloud and could have bitten her tongue when the words slipped out.

"I've been pondering the same thing," Bertie admitted.

"Me too," Cornelia said. "They've been friends for so long, I can't help but question why Maudie is here at Belle Haven instead of at Wanda Jean's house."

"My money's on the fact that Wanda Jean can't keep her mouth shut," Jillian said.

"And she isn't fond of dogs," Bertie said.

"That's true." Cornelia blew out a long, mournful breath.

"On Monday, Maudie up and left the bakery without Wanda Jean," Bertie reminded them.

"She was upset about finding Hugh and Della there," Jillian reminded her.

"Yes, but then Hugh and Maudie took off, and leaving Wanda Jean behind without so much as a glance."

"Let's not mention a word to Wanda Jean," Cornelia said. "She's a dear woman in her own way, but she likes to stir the pot more than anyone I know."

"We're all agreed on that," Jillian said. "In fact, all of Nathan County agrees with that, I'm sure."

"Bless her heart," Bertie added.

"We're wasting time with all this talk," Cornelia said, pulling her phone from the pocket of her skirt. "I personally made no promise not to call Hugh."

"Why, Aunt Cornelia, you can't—"

"I most certainly can, and I'm fixing to do it." She tapped the phone screen and held it to her ear. After a few moments, apparently the call went to voice mail. "Hi, Hugh. This is Cornelia. Where are you? Maudie is worried sick. We're worried sick. Would you call as soon as you get this message, please?" She tapped the end button on the screen and said, "Now we wait. And you call the hospital, Jillian. In fact, call all of the hospitals in the area." Her expression was so stern that Jillian knew there was no use in trying to convince her to wait for Hugh to respond.

Bertie and Cornelia watched and listened while she called every hospital within a hundred miles of Moss Hollow. None of them had any patients matching Hugh's description.

"I suppose we'll just have to see what tomorrow brings," Bertie said as Jillian disconnected her last call. "That's all we can do."

"No," Cornelia said. "We can call Coy Henderson."

Bertie shot her sister a withering glare. "No we cannot. Maudie expressly forbade it. Besides, we have nothing to suggest Hugh is in any imminent danger, so I don't think Coy would do a single thing."

Sheriff Henderson may not do a single thing, Jillian thought while her grandmother and great-aunt continued to bicker. *But if Hugh stays gone much longer, maybe I'd better.*

No word had come in from or about Hugh or Della by noon the next day, and Jillian's unease had blossomed into near panic. She took off her hairnet and apron, washed her hands, combed her hair, and told Bertie and Lenora that she needed to run an errand. She slipped out the bakery's back door and was nearly to her car when someone honked a car horn behind her.

Savannah pulled her vintage Buick Riviera up to Jillian and rolled down the driver's side window. "How did it go with Maudie yesterday? Is she okay this morning?"

Jillian glanced around to see if anyone could overhear, even though they were behind the bakery where the Dumpster sat. Customers rarely, if ever, ventured back there unless they'd taken a wrong turn at Puckett's Hardware next door. She refocused on Savannah. "What do you mean?"

"Maudie's staying at Belle Haven for a while, isn't she? At least until Hugh gets back, right?"

Jillian stepped closer to the red car's open window. "How'd you know about that?"

"I live in Moss Hollow," Savannah said as if it explained everything.

"I thought the only ones who knew she was at Belle Haven were those of us who live there."

Savannah scoffed. "You cannot seriously believe that. Hasn't anyone in the bakery said anything about it this morning?"

"Bertie and I have been working in the kitchen most of the time. Besides, we're making a concerted effort not to spread it around."

"I don't mean you and Bertie." Savannah rolled her eyes. "I mean the customers. Hasn't it been a hot topic of conversation?"

"If anyone said anything to Maggie while she was waiting on them, she never said a word."

"That's peculiar." Savannah stared at nothing for a few seconds, drumming her fingers on the steering wheel, lost in thought.

"Maggie is no gossip, you know," Jillian added.

"That's true." Savannah glanced at the keys in Jillian's hand. "So where are you going? And don't try to tell me you're out of sugar or eggs or something, because I can read you like a book. You're off to do some snooping, aren't you?"

Jillian heaved a sigh. Of course her best friend could take one look at her face and tell what she was thinking. And if Hugh's disappearing act and Maudie's flight to Belle Haven were common knowledge, then she saw no reason to be covert about her so-called snooping. "Truth be told, everything about this situation with Hugh and Maudie is peculiar. I'm going to go over to the Honeycutts' house."

"How come? Nobody's home, right?"

Jillian glanced around again. "I'm going to talk to Farris, if he's still there."

Savannah's brow creased. "I thought he and his wife went back to Wyoming yesterday." She stared at Jillian through narrowed eyes. "Apparently there are a few details the general population of Moss Hollow is ignorant of, including me."

Jillian wiggled her eyebrows. "Then you can come with me to Maudie's house. I'll even let you drive." She went around to the passenger side and got in.

Savannah made no move to put the car in gear. "Tell me what's going on."

A part of Jillian's mind still wrangled with her conscience, wanting to honor her agreement to keep the situation veiled. But another, more logical and pragmatic part of her knew Savannah's calm thinking would be invaluable for everyone concerned. Savannah could keep a secret and had enormous amounts of empathy for others. "Yesterday afternoon, Cornelia called me here at the bakery," she began, then filled Savannah in on everything that had happened since.

"Oh my," Savannah said when Jillian had finished. "That's a fine kettle of fish, for sure."

"Isn't it, though? So now I'm going to go talk with Farris, and I hope he can tell me what Maudie can't, or won't."

Concern filled Savannah's brown eyes. "I have to say, I'm worried about Hugh. I really think we should talk with Sheriff Henderson. What if there's been a car wreck somewhere that no one has reported?"

"I think this situation is serious, so I'm not opposed to talking to him at this point, in spite of Maudie's wishes. But before we take that step, let's see what Farris can tell us. Maybe he can clear everything up."

"All right. Let's go." Savannah pulled out of the back lot and followed the alley to the street. "Do you think Farris is still at their house? Maybe he went back to Wyoming."

Jillian shrugged. "Maudie said he was waiting for Della to come back."

"It's going on two days."

"A day and a half, if that. But I guess we'll find out soon enough whether he's there." They drove in silence for a minute, then Jillian mused aloud, "Maybe Della went home."

"Without Farris, and without telling anyone?" Savannah didn't sound convinced.

"I don't know. It's just a thought."

"I'm sure Farris would know if she went home. Surely he

called their house, or a neighbor, or a relative or someone. It'd be weird if he didn't."

"This whole situation is weird, remember?" Jillian said.

"And creepy. I mean, if Hunter disappeared, it's not like you'd say, 'Oh well, he probably ran off with someone.'"

Jillian shuddered at the mere thought. "I would move heaven and earth to find him, whether he ran off with someone or not. But he wouldn't do that. And besides, I'm not the jealous type who'd think such a thing."

Savannah shot her a cynical look. "Don't fool yourself. We all would think such a thing under the same circumstances. I would, and I have all the faith in the world in James."

The mere notion of Hunter leaving her for another woman turned the pit of Jillian's stomach into a block of ice. She shoved the disturbing image away, but the cold feeling stayed.

A few minutes later, they pulled into the driveway of Hugh and Maudie's white bungalow. The couple had lived there for as long as Jillian could remember. An uncomfortably sick feeling added to the chill in Jillian's stomach as she thought about either one no longer living there. She really, really hoped Maudie was wrong.

But if Maudie's wrong, then something must have happened to Hugh.

"That rental car is still here." Savannah dipped her head toward a blue compact car.

"Then maybe Della is here too. I wonder if Hugh has come home."

"Hugh's pickup isn't here."

Jillian winced. "I guess that means he's still gone."

"Or," Savannah said merrily, "maybe he returned, found out Maudie is at Belle Haven, and went out there to get her." Savannah's bright expression gave Jillian a foolish moment of hope before she added, "But I suppose if that were the case, Cornelia would have let you know."

The front door opened, and Farris stepped outside, watching their car expectantly. He approached with slow steps.

Savannah's face registered surprise. "Goodness, he looks a lot like Hugh, doesn't he? I never noticed the other night."

"He certainly does." Jillian chewed on her lower lip. "I wonder if Farris is harboring the same suspicions as Maudie."

"You mean that maybe Della and Hugh ran off together?"

"Yes. Honestly, Savannah, the very idea is so ludicrous it makes me dizzy." Jillian glanced toward the gray-haired man who approached, squinting hard trying to see them through the windshield. "We'd better get out. He seems anxious."

Farris halted halfway to the car, an uncertain smile on his face.

"Hello," Jillian said as she got out. "We met at the party the other night, briefly. I'm Jillian Green, and this is my friend, Savannah Wilson."

"Oh, sure. Yes, of course." Farris shook both their hands with great strength and warmth. "I believe I saw you at the bakery the other day too. Right?"

"You did."

His gaze shifted between Jillian and Savannah awkwardly. "I, uh, I don't suppose you've seen my wife lately?"

Savannah shook her head. "I'm sorry, no."

Jillian cleared her throat. "We're a little concerned, frankly, and we wanted to talk with you if that's all right."

The pain on Farris's face was so real and sharp that Jillian nearly flinched. He stiffly gestured toward the house. "Come inside. Everyone else has gone, and I'm just . . ." He shrugged, stuffed his hands in his pockets, then turned and led the way to the front door like a man defeated.

Jillian had never been inside the Honeycutts' house when it was completely quiet, and she found it rather creepy. The dogs were usually padding around, snuffling or panting, and getting in the way. Hugh nearly always had the television on to one of the sports networks while Maudie bustled around in the kitchen pouring coffee or sweet tea. And Wanda Jean was a daily guest who kept up a constant stream of chatter.

"Have a seat." Farris waved toward the living room sofa. "I'll get you some coffee."

"Please don't bother." Jillian sat down. "At least not for me."

"Me neither," Savannah said as she joined her.

"All right, then." Farris settled in an armchair. He sat forward, shoulders rounded, hands clasped between his knees. His eyes were full of misery.

"How are you, Mr. Honeycutt?" Jillian asked.

He made an impatient gesture with one hand. "It's just Farris, please. And I guess I'm doing as well as can be expected under the circumstances. What have you come here to tell me?"

Jillian shifted uneasily. "We haven't come here to tell you anything, I'm afraid."

He frowned and his back stiffened. "No? You mean you don't know where my family is?"

"Maudie is still in the area, if that helps," Savannah said. "But that's all we've got."

Farris nodded. "I know. She said she didn't think it was right for the two of us to be staying in the same house without our spouses, and she was going to go stay with friends in Bell Harbor or some such place. I have no idea where that is." As soon as he said it, dismay bloomed across his features. "That just slipped out. Please forget I said it, because she asked me not to tell anyone."

"She's at Belle Haven," Jillian said. "It's where I live with my grandmother and great-aunt."

His face cleared. "I see. So she's been with you. How is she?"

"She's upset. Worried and confused."

"She was in a right state when she left here," Farris said. "I told her I'd go to a hotel, but she told me she couldn't stay in a house where love had died. Said if Hugh did come home, she didn't want to be here to see him."

"Oh my. Poor Maudie." Savannah looked thoroughly torn.

"Yes, poor Maudie." Farris blew out a deep breath. "This whole mess is my fault, you know. Did she tell you?"

"What do you mean?" Jillian asked.

He gazed at them, as if measuring their ability to listen. "You came to talk to me, so—" A movement out the front room window caught his attention, and he stiffened and scowled. "Not again! I can't seem to get rid of that woman."

Jillian glanced outside and saw Wanda Jean scurrying up the front walk to the house. "Have you told her anything, Farris?"

He shook his head. "No. She came over earlier in the week, before Maudie left. They had words outside, and she didn't come back until yesterday. Maudie asked me not to talk to her, but she keeps popping up at the door. The first time, she just walked right in and got herself a cup of coffee like she owned the place. I've taken to locking the doors." He lowered his voice. "See? She's rattling the knob right now instead of knocking. What's wrong with her? Is she the town lunatic?"

Jillian grimaced. "She's Maudie's best friend."

"Oh? Maudie didn't say that. She just asked me not to talk to her."

"It seems they've had a falling-out," Savannah said, "but they've been so close for so long, I imagine she's as worried as the rest of us, if she knows Hugh is gone."

"In that case, should I let her in? Talk to her?" Farris made to stand.

"*No!*" Jillian and Savannah said together, so forcefully that the man jumped.

"I'll deal with Wanda Jean." Savannah hurried to the door. A moment later, she was outside and had the woman's arm in a firm grip, steering her back toward her car.

"Would you look at that." Farris's face broke into a small grin as he watched. "That girl knows her stuff."

"She does indeed." They watched for a moment as the pair stood near Wanda Jean's car and talked, then Jillian turned to Hugh's brother. "Farris, one thing I'd like to know, and please forgive me if I'm being nosy or inappropriate, but do you think your brother and your wife left together yesterday?"

He shrugged and shook his head. "I don't know. Appears that way, what with both of them being gone when we got up and neither of them coming back yet."

"Did you hear them stirring around? Maybe talking?"

"No ma'am."

"What about luggage? Did they take clothes with them?"

"I don't know if Hugh took anything. Our stuff was in suitcases and ready to go because we planned to go home yesterday. Della might have taken some things out of them, but the luggage is still here."

Farris seemed so blasé that Jillian felt compelled to ask, "Aren't you concerned?"

"A little, I guess. I'm more concerned about Maudie than anyone. Hugh taking off without a word surprised her, but not me. That's what he did before, y'know, a long time ago. Took off and never came back. But am I concerned about Della? Not really. She's always pretty much done what she wants, regardless."

"Regardless of what?"

"Of anyone else, or what they want, or what they need." He winced. "I know she's my wife, and I love her, so maybe I shouldn't be saying anything against her, but it's the truth. She's a free spirit. One of those artistic types. Did she lure Hugh away from Maudie?

It's possible. In fact, it's highly likely."

This information made the knot in Jillian's stomach clench tighter. A glance outside showed Wanda Jean and Savannah still talking intently. Wanda Jean seemed quite animated and made more than one attempt to come back to the house.

"Listen, Farris, it looks like I need to help Savannah." She started for the front door but paused. "Whatever you do, don't breathe a word of what you just told me to Wanda Jean."

"Of course. Not a word."

Jillian gave him a quick smile, then hurried outside to her friends. Wanda Jean was hollering loud enough that a couple of neighbors had come onto their porches to see what was going on. *What is that woman up to?*

"Jillian!" Wanda Jean shrieked, running up to her. Her silvery-gray bun wobbled on her head as if it would fall off.

Jillian put her arms out to catch the older woman. "Now, Wanda Jean, don't get so—"

"All I want to do is talk to Maudie and find out what's going on, but she won't return my phone calls, and no one will let me near her. Not Hugh's brother, and not even your best friend!" Wanda Jean gestured toward Savannah. "How would you feel if Savannah suddenly went silent on you and acted like she couldn't stand to breathe the same air you did? You'd leave no stone unturned to find out why, wouldn't you?"

Jillian frowned when Wanda Jean grabbed her arm. "There's no reason for you to—"

"Maudie hasn't answered her phone, or returned my messages, or texted me, or anything. I haven't seen her since Monday. That man"—she pointed at Farris watching them from the doorway—"refuses to let me inside the house. He has even slammed the door right in my face."

By this time, sweat was running down Wanda Jean's cheeks

like unchecked tears. Her face was alarmingly red, and her eyes were filled with fire.

"Let's calm down," Jillian said as soothingly as possible.

"I am not going to calm down!" Wanda Jean shouted. "Not until I get some answers. I need to know what's g-going on . . . becau—" Confusion leaped across her features and her eyes grew wide. She reached out, then she fell forward against Jillian.

Unable to bear the stricken woman's unexpected weight, Jillian toppled to the ground and was pinned beneath her. Although nearly breathless from the impact, Jillian managed to choke out to Savannah, "Call 911!"

9

Farris rushed to help Jillian out from under Wanda Jean while Savannah placed the call for help. After Jillian had scrambled to her feet, she and Farris worked together to turn Wanda Jean over on her back. Farris then motioned for Jillian to stand back.

She watched, panic-stricken, as Farris crouched over Wanda Jean to check her pulse and listen to her chest for sounds of breathing. Without a word, he began vigorous, rapid chest compressions. It seemed the world had stopped except for the sounds of Farris trying to save Wanda Jean's life, but in the distance, sirens shrieked as rescue approached.

The wails grew louder and louder until, a few moments later, a Nathan County Sheriff's cruiser pulled up, lights flashing, with Deputy Tom Shaw behind the wheel. An ambulance arrived right behind him, and three paramedics spilled out.

By this time, curious and concerned neighbors no longer stood at their front doors or on porches, but clustered in their yards near the sidewalk.

Farris continued CPR until the medics hustled over and two of them relieved him of his efforts. Another paramedic led Farris to the front steps, where she had him sit so she could check his vitals.

"What happened here?" Deputy Shaw asked as he approached Savannah and Jillian, who were standing a few feet away from where Farris sat.

"Wanda Jean was upset, and then she collapsed," Jillian said.

"What was she upset about?"

"Maudie," Savannah said.

Tom's eyebrows went up.

"They're having a few problems right now," Savannah explained.

"Oh?"

"Personal problems." Savannah shrugged, clearly trying not to air all the women's dirty laundry. "Nothing for law enforcement to be concerned about."

"Oh?"

Jillian wondered if nonchalance was one of Tom Shaw's favorite interviewing tactics. She knew for a fact that if Deputy Goodman "Gooder" Jones hadn't been on vacation, he'd have been on the scene, hammering Jillian and Savannah with questions faster than they could answer them. Gooder and Jillian had a relationship most similar to that of a brother and sister—siblings who bicker at any given chance but, in the end, have each other's backs. *This situation is tense enough. It's just as well Gooder's in Canada. Maybe they'll keep him.*

Conversation stopped as the paramedics secured Wanda Jean on the gurney and wheeled her to the ambulance. After the door closed with a *thunk* behind the third paramedic, who had apparently given Farris a clean bill of health, the vehicle sped off down the street toward the hospital.

"I can't help but think this was my fault." Farris's words immediately drew the deputy's interested gaze.

"It was not," Jillian said immediately, shaking her head.

"Please don't think that way," Savannah added.

Apparently Deputy Shaw wasn't as inclined to dismiss the older man's words. "What do you mean?" he asked.

Farris rubbed his temple. "I mean, I think I may have—"

Jillian glanced at the neighbors who lingered on the periphery. She refused to let them overhear whatever Farris was about to say. Besides that, he appeared to be shaken up and in need of a cool drink. "Let's go inside and get Farris settled," she said. "Then I'm going to the hospital if someone will give me a ride."

"I'll take you," Savannah said. "Farris, are you all right? You're looking pale."

"I'm fine." Farris got to his feet unsteadily. He led Jillian, Savannah, and Tom into the house, explaining on the way, "It's been a few years since I've needed my emergency skills, and I'm a little winded, that's all. The EMT took my vitals and checked me over. I'm okay. Really."

"You ought to sit down anyway." Jillian indicated the chair he'd used earlier. "We aren't leaving until you're comfortable."

"I'll just go get you something to drink," Savannah offered, then headed for the kitchen.

Farris sat, but got up immediately. "Maybe I should go with you to the hospital. After all, that woman wouldn't have collapsed if I had—" He sat down, hard, as if his legs couldn't support him.

"Stop blaming yourself." Jillian waved away his concerns. "All you did was talk to her."

Tom cleared his throat. "You say this was your fault. Tell me what you mean."

"Farris didn't do anything," Jillian protested. "Certainly nothing that warrants an interrogation."

Savannah returned from the kitchen and pressed a glass of cool water into the older man's hand. "That's right."

Tom's face remained serious. "I'd like him to answer anyway."

Farris met Shaw's gaze. "Someone asked me to keep a secret, and I kept it. That woman—Wanda Jean—has been badgering me for the details and got herself a little worked up when I refused to tell her what she wanted to know. Well, more than a little."

"Secret about what?" Tom's nonchalance seemed to be transforming into annoyance.

"It's nothing you need to know, Tom," Savannah said gently.

"But you all know it?" When none of them replied, the deputy added, "I hardly see how it's a secret if everyone knows it already."

"The thing is, everyone does *not* know it," Jillian said, "and it needs to stay that way. It's a private family matter."

"I see," Tom said, his tone quite clipped. "If this becomes something other than a private family matter and escalates into a public problem, I expect one of you to get in touch with me or someone else at the sheriff's department. Understood?"

Jillian couldn't help the smile that tugged at the corners of her mouth. "You have been hanging around with Gooder too long, Tom. I like you better when you're yourself."

A look of surprise flashed across his face, and then he gave her his crooked grin. "You could be right. He has a way of rubbing off on people, I reckon." He turned serious again. "You folks get in touch if it comes to that. All right?"

"Yes, of course we will." Jillian showed the deputy to the door. "Thanks, Tom."

"Is that cop going to cause trouble?" Farris asked after the cruiser was out of sight.

"Tom's not one to make trouble where there's none to be found," Savannah said.

Farris set his glass aside and got to his feet. "I'm going to the hospital. You girls coming with me?"

Jillian ran a quick, appraising gaze over him and thought he still seemed a little shaky. "Are you determined to go?"

Farris gave a sharp nod. "One hundred percent determined."

"I think it's best if you ride with us," Savannah said.

"That's fine. Just as long as I can make my peace with that poor woman before—well, you know. In case she passes."

The very idea horrified Jillian. She hadn't even stopped to think that Wanda Jean's life might actually be in danger. *First Hugh and Della disappear, and now Wanda Jean is headed to the emergency room. What next?*

Jillian rode in the Riviera's back seat on the way to the hospital, and she remained tense and worried for the entire drive. Her state of mind was reflected in her companions' silence and fidgets.

"Have you tried to contact your wife?" Savannah asked Farris at one point. He turned to stare at her as if he either had not heard or didn't understand. "Or does she not have a cell phone?"

"She has one. I dialed it a few times, but there's been no answer. I didn't expect one." Farris heaved a long sigh. "I tried calling our place in Wyoming, in case she'd gone home. If she's there, she didn't pick up the phone. But that's not unusual for Della. She just goes her own way without much regard for anyone else."

The man's near indifference regarding his wife's whereabouts troubled Jillian. "Do you have any idea where she might be?"

"I, uh . . ." He shook his head and stared down at his hands for a long moment. "I'm not up to talking about this right now, if you don't mind."

"We understand. We don't want to pressure you." Savannah glanced into the rearview mirror. "Do we, Jillian?"

Jillian met her friend's eyes in the mirror. "Of course not." *But if you know more than you're letting on, I'm not letting you stay quiet much longer.*

They made the rest of the drive in silence. Jillian studied the back of Farris's head and thought about how he and his brother looked so much alike from so many different angles. They shared a similar smile, the same heavy eyebrows, and the same tall, lean build. Even his neat gray hair sported a small cowlick on the right side of his neck just as Hugh's did.

What had happened all those years ago to tear the two men apart? It had been deep and serious enough that five decades of distance and silence had been unable to heal the wound for Hugh. Farris seemed less invested in the event that set things off than his brother. Farris might be willing to try to make things right between them. But if that was true, Jillian wondered, why had he not tried before now? *There's more to this, and I'm afraid it's darker than any of us think.*

Farris confused her. He seemed to harbor more concern for Maudie, and even Wanda Jean, than for his own wife. Why was that? Did he not care where she was or what had happened, or did he merely hide his feelings well? He'd indicated more than once that Della was a free spirit who didn't give much consideration to others, and that this situation was not out of the norm. But still, considering both his brother and his wife were missing, one would think he'd be at least a little anxious to find them.

Or was he like Maudie—too hurt, too confused, and too stubborn to try to get answers that might slice deeper into that wound?

And what about the estrangement between him and his brother? It was so long ago that surely time would have smoothed the raw edges.

Jillian shook her head as they turned into the hospital parking lot. *There simply has to be more to the story.*

They weren't allowed to see Wanda Jean, and no one on the staff at Nathan County Hospital would share much beyond confirming that she was a patient.

"What does that mean, 'She's being taken care of'?" Farris scowled at the nurse they'd asked for information. "Is she just lying back there, waiting to see a doctor? Is she in ICU? Is she having surgery? Is she—"

Jillian put one hand on his arm and tried to gently pull him away from the nurses' station. "As she told us, regulations forbid hospital staff from breaking patient confidentiality."

"I don't care about that. I want to know if she's alive and going to stay that way." Farris pinned a final flinty glare on the nurse, then turned to Jillian. "You know these people. Can't you make them tell us something?"

"Moss Hollow isn't quite that small, Farris." Jillian gave him a sympathetic look as she led him away from the desk, Savannah on their heels. "Even if I did know the staff, it's not likely they'd risk their jobs by breaking the rules for me or anyone else."

He made an impatient gesture and stalked even farther away from the nurses' station. For a moment, Jillian thought he was going to storm through a door that clearly read *No Admittance*.

He pivoted and returned to where Jillian and Savannah stood. "Where's her family?" he asked. "They'll know something."

"Wanda Jean is a widow," Savannah said, "and she doesn't have any kids."

Farris took this in. "Right. I remember Maudie telling me that. But surely there's someone, somewhere, who can tell us something."

The woman behind the desk was eyeing him with suspicion and speaking quietly to someone on the phone. Did she think Farris posed a threat? Had she called security? She hung up and called to him.

"We're looking into this for you, Mr. Honeycutt," she said. "Please have a seat, and someone will be with you soon."

He gave a short nod. "Thank you."

They sat in the waiting area for what seemed an eternity, thumbing through magazines, watching news and weather updates on the muted television, or checking their phones. Farris glanced up every few seconds and frowned toward the desk, tapping his foot impatiently.

"She should've stayed home," he muttered. "That's all that I asked of her. 'Stay home.' Simple as that."

"That doesn't surprise me." Savannah flipped another page of the cooking magazine she was reading. "Wanda Jean Maplewood has never been one to simply stay home."

Farris blinked at her as if he had no idea what she was talking about, then his face cleared. "Oh, her. Well, if she'd stayed home and minded her own business, then maybe none of this would have happened. But I was talking about Della."

He got up and paced the length of the room several times, finally pausing in front of Jillian and Savannah. "How about some coffee or a cold drink? I saw some vending machines outside."

"Nothing for me, thanks," Jillian said.

Savannah shook her head. "Me neither, but thank you."

Farris left the room, digging in his pants pocket for money. When he was out of earshot, Jillian murmured to Savannah, "Do you think he's all right?"

"He seems a little pale. And he's probably terribly worried."

"Yes, but I'm sure there's something else. Don't you agree?"

Savannah scrutinized her face for a moment. "Like what?"

"I think he's holding something back."

"It's as plain as day that he feels guilty about what happened to Wanda Jean. Maybe this curious behavior is how he deals with guilt."

"Maybe." Jillian caught sight of Farris returning to the waiting area. "Here he comes."

Farris ambled over to where the women sat, a cup of coffee in his hand and candy bars in his shirt pocket. "Ladies, I realize I've been a little testy with you," he said as he sat down. "I apologize. I get cranky if I don't eat. It's my blood sugar, you see." He set the coffee on the magazine table next to him, then retrieved the candy bars from his pocket and held them out. "I have chocolate, peanut butter, and chocolate caramel. Take your pick."

"Just what I needed. Thank you." Jillian gratefully accepted the caramel. Neither she nor Savannah had eaten lunch, and biting through the dark chocolate into soft caramel helped smooth some of the raw edges created by the morning's events.

Savannah chose the peanut butter, and Farris opened the chocolate bar. He lost his edginess quickly after he ate, leaving him in a seemingly better frame of mind. They chatted about the weather for a few minutes, but they were interrupted when a middle-aged woman in a dark business suit and low-heeled black shoes approached them.

"Which of you women is Ms. Green?" the professional woman asked.

Jillian looked up, surprised. "That's me."

"I'm Pru Thompson, assistant PR coordinator. I understand there has been some concern about Mrs. Maplewood?"

"That's right," Jillian said. "We were there when she collapsed."

"Please come with me, Ms. Green." Ms. Thompson gestured toward the door. Farris and Savannah started to stand up too, but the woman shook her head. "Just Ms. Green."

"Okay." Jillian followed Ms. Thompson out of the room and

down a corridor into a small office.

"Have a seat." The woman pointed to a narrow pale-green chair as she settled behind the desk. Opening a file, she read silently for a few moments, then met Jillian's gaze. "Mrs. Maplewood has given us permission to divulge her medical information to you."

"What about the others?"

Ms. Thompson shook her head. "Just you."

Jillian thought this was odd, but right then, all she cared about was Wanda Jean's health. "How is she?"

The woman closed the folder, then she clasped her hands and set them on top. "She had a heart attack. She is lucky that someone nearby knew CPR."

"That was Farris, the man I was sitting with in the waiting room."

The woman lifted her eyebrows. "Was it? I thought it had been you. At any rate, we're keeping her here for a while."

"What else can you tell me?"

"Right now, given her condition, she's doing as well as can be expected. She's awake, lucid, talkative. Very talkative."

Jillian nearly smiled at that. *Good old Wanda Jean.* "Can we see her?"

Ms. Thompson shook her head. "Not until after our cardiologist examines her, and perhaps not even then."

"But once she's stronger?"

"I'm not sure. You see, she's already said she wants no visitors, even when she's allowed to have them. She's quite adamant about it."

Jillian sat back in her chair and frowned. "None? But that's so unlike Wanda Jean. She's very social."

"This is an unusual circumstance for her. And it's her decision."

"I find that hard to believe."

Ms. Thompson shrugged, keeping her expression blank. "We don't lie. Not to our patients. Not to the public."

"I'm sorry," Jillian said. "I didn't mean to imply that you were lying. It's just that I find it hard to believe Wanda Jean wouldn't even want to talk to Maudie Honeycutt, her best friend."

The woman gave her thin smile. "She said no one." She opened the folder and scanned it again. "I do need to ask one thing. Do you know if Mrs. Maplewood has been under a lot of stress lately?"

Jillian nodded. "She has. Do you think stress is the reason she had the heart attack?"

"That's not for me to say." The woman made a note and returned her gaze to Jillian. "Is there anything more you can tell us?"

Jillian thought quickly. If she were going to share any more information about Wanda Jean and her state of mind, it should be with a bona fide doctor, not an assistant to someone in public relations.

"When will her doctor be here?"

"He's a very busy man."

"I'm sure he is." Jillian wasn't in the mood to back down.

"You want to talk to him?" The woman's voice made it sound to Jillian as if she thought no one in the history of medicine had ever wanted to consult a physician.

"I do," Jillian said firmly.

"I'll see what I can arrange."

Bertie greeted Jillian with a question as soon as she walked in the back door of the bakery. "Where have you been?"

Jillian slipped on an apron and gave her grandmother an apologetic smile. "I'm sorry. Something came up."

Lenora joined them, and both older women put their fists on

their hips and studied her as if she were a dirty spot on the floor.

"Something came up and you had to take a three-hour lunch break?" Bertie's eyebrows were practically to her hairline. "You never called us, and you don't look any worse for wear, so it clearly wasn't much of an emergency."

"Actually, it was an emergency." Jillian took a breath. "Wanda Jean had a heart attack."

Their mouths dropped open in twin expressions of shock.

"What? When? Is she okay?" Lenora asked.

Bertie crossed her arms. "Why didn't you call?"

Jillian held up her hands to ward off the battery of questions. "I'm sorry I didn't call. I had other things on my mind, and I just didn't think. For starters, she's stable. She's at the Nathan County Hospital."

"We should go see her," Bertie said, starting to untie her apron. "And why are you shaking your head at me?"

"She won't see any visitors."

Lenora scowled. "No visitors?"

"None."

Bertie laid one hand against her chest, as if checking her own heartbeat. "Is her condition that bad?"

"I don't know."

Bertie huffed. "You were right there at the hospital, weren't you? Why didn't you ask?"

"I did ask," Jillian said defensively. "I had to practically beg to talk with a doctor, and when he finally came to talk to me, he basically told me what the PR person said."

"Which was?"

Jillian ticked off each item on her fingers. "That she'd had a heart attack, that she was in serious but stable condition at the moment, that they were keeping a close eye on her, that the cardiologist would be seeing her when he was out of surgery, that she can't have visitors, and that someone will call me." Her gaze went from Bertie to Lenora and back again. "That is all I know, so there is no reason under the shining sun for the two of you to look at me like that. When someone calls me, I'll let you know, okay? There's nothing else we can do."

After several tense moments, Bertie finally blew out a long, loud breath. "Mercy on us," she muttered. "I'll call the pastor and get a prayer chain started. Which I could've done before now if you'd just called from the hospital like you should have. What on earth did you have on your mind that was so important it blotted out all good sense?"

"Hugh and Maudie, mostly."

Bertie paused with her hand on the bakery phone and leveled a gaze at Jillian. "Seems to me that family's problems have set off a wave of trouble in this town. I just hope Hugh gets himself back here and fixes this mess before anyone else lands in the hospital."

That evening, Maudie refused to come down to supper. Cornelia sent Jillian up with a tray, but Maudie called for her to leave it outside the door. Jillian hesitated, but did as she was asked.

"Likely as not, she's feeling guilty for ignoring her friend for the last few days," Cornelia said when Jillian returned to the kitchen and shared Maudie's request.

"I'm sure that's part of it anyway." Jillian sighed as she sat down to her own plate at the kitchen table. "This salad looks delicious, Cornelia." She speared a bite of greens and ate it, appreciating the complementary zing of the lemon-herb vinaigrette. Much as she appreciated rich comfort food like the chicken and dumplings her aunt had prepared as the main course, she also appreciated a good salad, which had been a staple in her life when she'd lived in California. That was mostly because it was one of the few dishes she'd been able to prepare. She smiled at how much had changed in the few years since she'd moved home.

"Thank you, dear." Cornelia beamed. "Fresh yellow peppers and heirloom tomatoes right off the vine today."

Bertie stopped before taking her own first bite. "You ought to slow down so you can taste the meal, Jillian."

Jillian realized she had been eating a bit quickly. "Sorry, I'm meeting Savannah soon and I need to get a move on."

Cornelia narrowed her eyes and studied Jillian's face. "Why?"

"We have a little something to do." After everything that had happened earlier, Farris had been too tired to discuss the situation concerning Hugh and Della any further. When she and Savannah had dropped Farris off at his brother's house, Jillian asked if they could return that evening. He'd hemmed and hawed for a bit but finally agreed.

"Don't be secretive," Bertie said. "I'll wait up for you and ask you again at midnight if I have to."

"And I'll sit up with her. I can tat those new curtains for my bathroom while I'm waiting. Bertie, do you think I should use that pale-pink thread or the minty-green thread? I have both those colors in my shower curtain."

"It doesn't matter."

"Of course it matters. I don't want to be stuck with something I might not like—"

"Cornelia, please hush. Right now, I want Jillian to tell us what's going on. We can talk about thread later."

Cornelia simmered for a moment, then relaxed and took a bite of salad.

Jillian had hoped to slip away from Belle Haven quietly and

without interrogation, but she knew her grandmother and great-aunt would do exactly as they had threatened, and the last thing she wanted to do was have this conversation late at night. It was better to fess up now. "We're going to Maudie's house."

"Mercy on us!" Cornelia's fork clattered to her plate. "You're going to break into her house? You've been raised better than that."

"We are *not* breaking into her house, Aunt Cornelia. Farris is still there, remember? We're going to go see him."

"You're going to talk to him?" Bertie asked.

"That's the plan," Jillian said.

"Is he expecting you?" Bertie asked. When Jillian nodded, she peppered her with another question. "What are you going to talk to him about?"

"We're just going to see if he has any ideas about what happened to Hugh and Della. He hinted around at some things this afternoon but didn't give us much information." Jillian glanced at her watch and got to her feet. "I'd better go. If you want to leave the dishes, I'll do them when I get home."

Cornelia looked outraged at the mere thought. "I have never left supper dishes sitting around in my entire life, and I don't intend to start now. But thank you for the offer."

Jillian gave Cornelia a peck on the cheek, then did the same to Bertie. Her grandmother grasped her arm. "You let us know exactly what you find out about Hugh."

"I will," Jillian promised. "If there's anything more to tell."

11

"I think James was hinting at coming along," Savannah said without preamble as she got into Jillian's white Prius a short while later. "But I told him he might scare Farris off. Don't you think?"

"Given how skittish Farris seemed before we left him this afternoon, you bet I agree. If we brought a stranger with us, he'd clam up faster than a coral reef."

"Glad we're on the same page." Savannah fastened her seat belt.

Jillian put the car in gear and pulled onto the street. "With all this secrecy and drama, doesn't it feel like we're living in a soap opera?"

"It's almost like a bad dream, isn't it? Except we're wide awake, there is no television, and Hugh and Della's disappearance is very real, whatever caused it." Savannah shuddered. "It gives me the creepiest feeling, to be honest. I feel like any minute somebody's going to jump out at us."

"Do you?" Jillian sent her best friend a curious look. "I don't feel that way at all. I just feel like the truth is being hidden because it's ugly."

Savannah grimaced. "Do we really want to know the ugly truth?"

"I think we *need* to know it, even if we don't *want* to know it."

"You do realize that depending on what we find out from Farris, we may need to talk to Sheriff Henderson even though Maudie doesn't want us to."

"I've been thinking about that."

"And?"

"Let's jump off that bridge when we get to it." Jillian turned onto the Honeycutts' street.

"Aren't we just supposed to cross bridges in your metaphor? I'm already nervous enough without you bringing death-defying stunts into the mix."

As she pulled into the driveway Jillian sent her friend what she hoped was a carefree grin—not necessarily because she didn't feel the same sense of anxiety, but because she was trying to tamp down her own nerves so they could present themselves as cool and casual to Farris. "It's because our adrenaline is pumping. And let's not forget we're doing this for our friends. If Farris can give us enough information to figure out where Hugh might be, then maybe we can settle everything."

"And everyone can live happily ever after," Savannah added. "I hope you're right."

Farris greeted them with a hesitant smile and invited them inside to sit down. He sat, but not with ease. He was always peering at either Jillian or Savannah, as if he were expecting them to create a problem.

"It's a lovely evening, isn't it?" Savannah asked as she settled into an armchair. "The lightning bugs will be all aglow as soon as the sun sets."

He nodded. "I like to see fireflies. We don't have them in Wyoming, so it's been years since I've had the pleasure. And we don't have this heat and humidity. I'm not quite used to it."

Savannah chuckled. "I've lived in Georgia all my life, and I don't think I'll ever get used to it."

"At least you have it nice and cool in the house," Jillian said. "Thank goodness for air-conditioning."

"When the sun goes down at home, the air gets pleasant," Farris said. "We don't use the air conditioner much at night."

They chatted about the climate and indulged in other small talk until Jillian sensed Farris finally relaxing. "Are you feeling better, Farris?" she asked.

"Better?"

"After the events of this afternoon, I mean. That was pretty upsetting."

"Oh. It was upsetting, but I'm fine, thank you." He fell silent, except for clearing his throat a few times. "I tested my blood sugar a bit ago, and it's good, so I'm—I'm just fine."

"I'm glad to hear that," Savannah said kindly.

"Me too." Jillian glanced at Savannah, then decided to launch into the reason they'd come over. "Farris, we're awfully worried about both Hugh and Maudie."

"I know."

Jillian leaned forward in her chair. "Aren't you?"

Unlike earlier, now Farris wouldn't make eye contact with either Jillian or Savannah. Instead, he examined his hands, which were clasped in his lap. "Yeah, I guess I am. Now."

"Now?" Jillian was confused. "But haven't you been concerned before now?"

"I don't know them very well," Farris said in a voice that sounded a lot to Jillian like he was trying to convince himself of something. "It could be that they fuss and separate with each other a lot."

Savannah's brow wrinkled. "Hugh is your brother, but you say you don't know him well."

"I mean, I used to, of course. But after a half a century, I'm not sure anymore."

"So you two really haven't been in touch in all that time?" Jillian asked. At Farris's nod, she added, "Did you ever reach out to him?"

Farris said nothing for a few moments, then raised his head. "Yeah, I did. On Christmas, about a year or two after it happened, I called him. He hung up the instant he heard my voice."

"You said 'after it happened,'" Savannah repeated. "After what happened, Farris?"

He shifted in his chair. "Well, after Della and I got married, Hugh was likely to have killed us both if he ever saw us again."

Jillian's eyes immediately went wide. "Hugh said that?"

Farris gestured in a half shrug, half nod.

"That doesn't sound like the Hugh Honeycutt we know," Savannah said.

"Not at all." Jillian shook her head. "He's kind and considerate, very low-key."

Farris shrugged. "I guess he's changed then."

"Were you hesitant about coming to Moss Hollow?" Jillian asked.

"Sure I was. Who wouldn't be? But Della insisted. She said she'd come by herself if she had to. I couldn't let her face Hugh by herself."

"Were you afraid he'd . . . ?" Jillian couldn't even finish her question. In her wildest dreams, she couldn't imagine Hugh behaving in any way that was remotely frightening.

"Afraid he'd become violent? You bet I was!" Farris's eyes flashed. "He said he would. My little brother never made idle threats or promises."

"Then you should have stayed home." Jillian squared her shoulders. "Both of you."

Farris pinned a hard look on Jillian. "Don't you think I tried to convince her of that? Della wouldn't listen. She's never listened, and she never will." He ran one hand over his head. "So I gave in and came with her. I'd hoped the years had mellowed him. When we got here, Maudie explained how she wanted us to be the big surprise at the party, her gift for him. So we stayed at the Southern Peach Inn. She spent quite a bit of time visiting with us there. I thought she was really friendly and sweet. She had such good things to say about Hugh, their son, their grandsons, and their life here in Moss Hollow. I figured he had changed. I was glad my brother had such a great woman in his life." He gave a short-lived smile. "She never mentioned our estrangement, which I thought was peculiar. Wouldn't you think most people in her situation would've asked about what had caused the split between us?"

Given that Maudie liked gossip and juicy details, Jillian agreed with him. "Didn't you bring it up?"

Farris shook his head. "I figured Hugh must have explained it all to her long ago, and it didn't matter to her. She didn't seem the least bit jealous."

"Jealous?" Savannah asked.

He nodded. "Of Della."

The ugly notions that had been lurking in the back of Jillian's mind, the ones she didn't want to give credence to, came creeping out of the dark corners and into her consciousness. She caught Savannah's eye and knew her friend had been harboring the same thoughts. She cleared her throat and forced herself to ask what she didn't want to. "Are you telling us that he and Della were more than just a singing duo?"

Farris stared at her in surprise. "Didn't you know?"

"Know?" Savannah echoed weakly.

He shifted in the chair and looked more uncomfortable than ever. "That's been the big problem all this time. I thought you already knew all about it. I thought everybody knew, or at least guessed the truth. Maybe I just ought to hush now."

"Farris, just say it." Jillian was done beating around the bush. "I do not want to be speculating at this point."

"Della and I eloped three days before their wedding date." The words rushed out of Farris as though he'd been waiting to say them for five days. Or fifty years.

"Whose wedding?" Jillian pressed, although she was fairly certain she knew exactly whose wedding he was referring to.

"Hugh and Della's, of course." A flush darkened his face, and he met Jillian's gaze like an embarrassed child. "We fell in love hard, Della and me."

"Apparently," Savannah murmured. "So why didn't she just break up with Hugh instead of running away from him?"

"For one thing," Farris said, "my brother was known all over town as a hothead with a hair-trigger temper, and most girls don't like that. At least they didn't back in my day."

"Hugh with a hot temper." Jillian shook her head. "I can't wrap my brain around that."

"It's the truth," he said defensively. "And another thing you should know: Della was my girl first."

"She was?" the women chorused, gaping at him.

"She sure was. We met at college, a small school in the Missouri Bootheel, and you better believe it was love at first sight. I wasn't too bad-looking in those days, and she was this tiny, pretty thing with blonde curls all the way to her waist. She had the biggest, brightest, bluest eyes of any I'd ever seen, before or since. First chance I got, I took her home to meet my folks in St. Charles." His smile was wistful, but it vanished with his next words. "Hugh is my kid brother by a couple of years, and he and Della hit it off right away. They were full of energy and big dreams, and they were both crazy about music. Music of all kinds, but especially country music. Rock and roll was the thing back then, you know. That's what kids of my generation were drawn to, not the down-home country music those two liked."

Farris paused for a moment, but Jillian urged him to continue. "Go on."

"So I guess you could say that when Hugh and Della met, they filled a void for each other. Della lived on the other side of St. Louis from us, in Belleville, so we visited back and forth a lot that summer. She and Hugh sang in church together sometimes. They liked those old country hymns like 'I'll Fly Away' and 'Rock of Ages.' I'll be the first to admit they were good. Pretty soon, word got around about them, and they were asked to sing at weddings and parties and such. By the end of the summer, she was his girl, not mine."

Savannah bit her lower lip, her eyes brimming with compassion. "That's a sad story, Farris. But you and Della got back together. Obviously."

"We did. But not until the two of them had what appeared to be the start of a music career a couple of years later." He swallowed hard, as if close to tears. "And you know what? I wanted Della to be happy. Singing with Hugh made her happy, so even before we got back together, I forgave him for taking her from me."

"That was good of you," Savannah said.

"Here's the thing, though: Hugh has not forgiven me, even after all these years, and even though she was my girl to begin with." Farris shifted his gaze between Jillian and Savannah, as though seeking enlightenment. "I fail to grasp why. I mean, I understood how angry he was right after it happened, but it's been so many years now."

"Sometimes it's hard to let go of a grudge, especially after a deep hurt," Jillian said quietly.

"But he's gone on to have such a great life," Farris said. "Maudie is a lovely woman. It's obvious how much she loves my brother and how devoted she is to him. Seems like that would account for something, you know? But he has spoken to me maybe twice since we got here, and that was to say 'hello' at the party, and 'excuse me' when we nearly bumped into each other in the hallway."

"That sounds awkward," Savannah said sympathetically.

Farris rubbed his hands together. "Funny thing is, he appears to have forgiven Della. You saw that for yourselves, didn't you? They got along just fine the night of the party."

"They seemed to," Jillian said, although she was hesitant to declare anything for certain about this situation. Farris's description of Hugh didn't match anything in Jillian's memory of Maudie's kind, gentle husband.

"Believe me when I say they got along better and better as time went on." Farris's voice had taken on a bitter twinge. "And another thing—they still sound good together when they sing. Not like the rusty voices you might expect from old folks."

"It's too bad the broken romance broke up the music," Savannah said.

Farris gave a short, humorless laugh. "Della wanted them to keep trying to reach their dream. Oh, how she wanted to. And she thought they would, that there wouldn't be any problem with them being together and singing. I had hoped she was right and she could have gone on with her pursuit, but I should have known better."

"It seems to me," Savannah said, "that the two of them being together after you and she got married might have been more than a little uncomfortable."

Farris pinned a hard look on her. "It seemed that way to Hugh too. Obviously. He took off when we came back from our honeymoon. That was the last time I saw him until the party."

Silence fell. While Farris seemed to drift and lose himself in his memories, Jillian processed what he'd said. The more she thought about the situation, the more uneasy she became. He'd told them it was the last time he had seen Hugh, but was it the last time Della had seen him? "Farris, do you think Della and Hugh left together?" she asked quietly.

"Yes."

That the two old friends, who'd been more than just friends and singing partners, had reunited, then left together at the same time made sense. But Jillian had known Hugh for as long as she could remember. She had a hard time embracing the concept if it involved him, no matter how much sense it made.

"Do you know where they are?" Savannah asked.

Farris shook his head.

Again, Jillian sensed he knew more than he was telling. "Do you know where they *might* be?"

He ran a hand over his head again and shifted in the seat, his face pinched and anxious. "I suppose they could have gone to Nashville again."

Jillian raised her eyebrows. "Really? Why?"

"Because in all the years since, Della has never stopped talking about Nashville—the Grand Ole Opry and all that. If the two of us hadn't run off and gotten married, they would've gone there and met with a record producer. They had it scheduled. And then Della and I . . ." Farris released a defeated sigh.

"But that was fifty years ago," Jillian said. "Surely neither of them believes they could still have that career."

"They sounded just as good as ever at the party," Farris said, almost defensively.

"Yes, they did," Savannah said. "But it seems a little far-fetched."

Farris held up one hand. "I know exactly what you're saying. They are too old to go chasing after that worn-out dream, and I agree. But Della has never let it go."

"She still wants a music career?" Jillian asked.

"Yep. Still thinks she's Dolly Parton." Farris shrugged. "She always believed she was an undiscovered star. Still does. Back in the day, I guess she was right, and I felt bad about it never happening for her."

He stopped speaking for a bit, a frown creasing his forehead as he stared at his hands. Savannah appeared to be ready to say something, but Jillian nonchalantly motioned for her to wait.

Farris soon continued. "A few years ago, Della wanted to try out for that TV show, *American Voice*. Got all excited about it and went online to sign up. But the rules set the contestants' age as no older than twenty-five. That's because the record companies and agents need time to help build careers, but she didn't understand that. She called up the network and tried to stir things up, but she wasn't allowed to audition. That was pretty hard on her. She went away for a while after that."

"Went away?" Jillian asked. "Where did she go?"

He shrugged. "Wherever it was she always went to when she'd leave."

Savannah frowned. "You never asked?"

"Sure I did. But she'd never tell me a thing, so I quit asking."

A short silence fell, then Jillian said what was on her mind. "If she was so determined, why didn't she try to succeed without Hugh? As a young woman, she was probably a powerhouse."

Farris scoffed and let his gaze travel out the window to stare at nothing.

"Didn't she try to go solo?" Jillian asked. "Or maybe find another singing partner?"

He shook his head and rubbed his palms against each other.

"Did you encourage her to try it on her own?" Savannah asked.

He shifted in his chair and cleared his throat. "Sure I did, but our life wasn't—that is, there wasn't much time or opportunity for such pursuits where we moved to. Or money either, for that matter."

"You moved away from St. Louis?" Jillian wondered how many more layers there were to this yarn.

"We wanted to see the country and we needed work, and we needed to get away from those who tried to make us feel bad about what we'd done. So we went west and hired out as ranch hands and property caretakers. There was plenty of work to keep us busy and paid, plenty of moving around, meeting new folks, living in new places to help satisfy some of Della's restlessness." He gave a wistful smile. "She did really well, and folks loved her.

Everyone has always loved Della, you know. She's got that kind of presence, all friendly and positive."

"But she never lost her dream of being a singer," Jillian said.

"Right. I'd catch her staring out the window, engrossed in her thoughts, and I knew what she was thinking and how she was feeling. She'd just up and disappear for a few hours or a few days, and when she'd get back, the restlessness would be gone out of her for a time."

"Didn't it worry you when she'd suddenly leave like that?" Jillian asked.

"Of course it did. The first few times anyway. Scared me. But after a while, I stopped letting it bother me too much. I knew she was taking care of herself the best way she could. And she always came back."

Savannah tipped her head to one side, a small frown puckering her forehead. "But what was she doing while she was gone?"

He shrugged.

"She never told you?"

"Nope. She never told me where she went, and she never said what she was doing while she was gone. It didn't do a bit of good to ask her about any of it because she'd never give a satisfying answer."

Jillian leaned forward, meeting his eyes. "But Farris, didn't you ever try to find her? Go after her and see where she was going, what she was doing?"

He fidgeted a bit, then stood. "Excuse me, but I need some coffee. I'll fix a fresh pot for all of us."

When they heard the sounds of coffee being made, Savannah whispered, "This is one of the oddest relationships I've ever heard of."

Jillian nodded. "She leaves him without a word, over and over, and she still believes she could become famous. It's almost like the words to a country song, isn't it?"

"Maybe she decided if she couldn't sing it, she could live it."

Jillian shot a glance toward the kitchen. "I believe Farris knows more than he's telling."

"This is hard on him," Savannah said. "He may not want to share much more."

"And he's really said nothing that will help us find Della and Hugh."

"I know, but I see how he might think the two of them went off together."

"As much as I hate the idea, it seems more and more possible to me. But think about it, Savannah. The Hugh Honeycutt you and I have known all our lives has never shown the least sign of being restless or unhappy with Maudie, or with Moss Hollow. So why, after all these years and this wide separation between him and his brother, would he up and leave with Della?"

Savannah tapped one finger against her chin, lost in thought. "You know, it's possible that all this time, Hugh and Maudie have been living an entirely different life when no one else was around."

Her statement made sense, and Jillian felt sick just considering it. "I really don't want to believe that."

"Neither do I, but it's something we should consider. It *is* possible."

"Don't you think Wanda Jean would have noticed it, if that were the case?"

Savannah blew out a long breath, her expression troubled. "She never misses a thing, that's for sure. But seeing as how she and Maudie are so close, she might have decided not to mention it."

Farris returned from the kitchen with a tray holding three mugs full of black coffee. It looked strong enough to keep Jillian awake all night, but she and Savannah each took a cup and thanked him. He sat down, blew on it a few times, then took a careful sip.

"I suppose it's likely those two are together," he said. "Maybe in Nashville, like I said earlier, but it's just as possible they aren't.

When Della gets the restless urge, she doesn't want anyone hanging onto her. She doesn't want to answer to anyone or be responsible for anyone." He cleared his throat. "If he left with her, there's a fifty-fifty chance he's not with her now."

"Farris!" Jillian set her mug down on the coffee table a little harder than she meant to. "If that's the case, why didn't you say so earlier?"

His face reddened. "Because I don't know anything," he argued. "I can't tell you what you want to know, because I don't know anything, and I'm tired of trying to figure it all out." He sagged back in his chair and bowed his head.

"Farris, we came to you because we are *worried* about them," Savannah said.

He lifted his gaze to meet hers. "I know you are. You've told me several times."

These words pricked Jillian's confusion and turned it into annoyance. Did this man always roll over and accept fate? Was the day he eloped with Della the only time he'd ever taken initiative? In all the years since, had he ever stood up for himself?

"What else can you tell us?" Jillian asked. "What about your cousins, Sheldon and Starla? Do you think they might have some information?"

He shook his head. "I doubt it. Why would they?"

"Because they're your family," Jillian said more sharply than she intended.

"Have you called them?" Savannah asked. "Or been in touch with any of your friends in Wyoming, to see if they've heard from Della?"

"Not really."

Jillian scowled. "What's that mean? Either you have, or you haven't."

Farris blew out a long, slow breath and said, "I'm tired. Let's call it a night."

Jillian stiffened and started to retort, but Savannah spoke first. "Of course you're tired, and we understand that. Don't we, Jillian?"

It took Jillian a few seconds to swallow her irritation. "Yes. We understand. It's been a long, hard day for all of us. But before we go, do you have your cousin's phone number?"

Farris nodded, took out his wallet and withdrew a white business card edged in gold. "You can keep that. I have another two just like it at home. They come to see us every so often, believe it or not."

"Why wouldn't we believe it?" Savannah asked sweetly.

He made a dismissive gesture. "They aren't much for Starla's side of the family, which is what I am. They have to pass through Sheridan where we live to get to their oldest son up in Billings. They stop by our place out of family obligation, not because they want to see us."

"I'm sorry you feel that way," Savannah said. "You seem like such a nice guy."

He raised his eyebrows as if her remark surprised him. His smile erased the haunted look in his eyes and took years off his face. "I try to be a nice guy." The smile faded. "But I don't always succeed."

"Trying is more than some people are willing to do," Savannah assured him.

He gave a brief nod but said nothing.

Jillian's irritation was not so easily soothed. It was crystal clear that Farris had more to say, but she was pretty sure she'd never get it out of him. "What about Della's phone number?" she asked. "You said she has a cell phone?"

"She does, but she doesn't turn it on unless she's using it. I can't ever reach her on it. Don't even know why she has the silly thing." He took a pen from his shirt pocket and wrote her number on the back side of Starla's card.

Or maybe she just doesn't answer when Farris is calling. The thought popped so unexpectedly into Jillian's head that she twitched a little.

"Go ahead and make your calls if you want to," Farris said, "but I think you're wasting your time. And Sheldon and Starla won't know anything. They left the party early, and left Moss Hollow the next morning. And as for Della, if she answers or returns the call, I'll be surprised."

"We'll at least give it a shot," Jillian said.

He stood and walked to the door, a less-than-subtle indicator that their meeting was over.

"Thank you for your time," Savannah said as she stepped outside. "We'll let you know what we find out."

"I'd appreciate it," he said.

"And if you think of anything else, would you call me, please?" Jillian forced a smile.

"Of course." By that time, the sun was nothing more than a pale glow on the western horizon. As they reached the car, he called out, "Good night, and thank you for caring." He closed the front door and turned off the porch light, thrusting them into the darkness of the evening.

Jillian didn't move. "Savannah?"

"Yes?"

"Why do you think he's still here instead of going back to Wyoming?"

"He's waiting for Della to come back to Moss Hollow, isn't he?"

"I don't know. Is he?" Jillian climbed into the car.

"All I know is that Farris Honeycutt is a strange man." Savannah buckled her seat belt, clearly ready to get away from the bungalow.

Instead of starting the car, Jillian stared through the windshield at the dark house. "I feel like we have taken a giant step backward."

"You're just overwhelmed by the day's events and what we've learned up to this point," Savannah said. "All we have to do is discuss what we now know and create our plan of action."

"Maybe you're right." Jillian started the car. "I was hoping he'd say something like 'I'm pretty sure Della went to visit her sister in Waycross, and Hugh went on a short trip to Memphis to hear the blues.'"

In the light from the dashboard control panel, Savannah's cynical expression was easy to read.

"I suppose you weren't expecting a solid lead," Jillian said.

"Certainly not the kind you just spouted." Savannah bit her lip, then said slowly, "You may not want to hear this, but I think it's time to talk to Sheriff Henderson, whether Maudie wants us to or not." The words hung between them, nearly visible and flashing. "It's been almost two days."

"You may be right, Savannah, but I don't like what involving the sheriff implies about this whole situation. It just makes everything seem that much more serious. As serious as a heart attack—and then some."

Jillian drove to the plain brick building that housed the sheriff's department and parked in the lot, which was empty except for two cruisers. Talking to the law was the right thing to do at this point, she knew, no matter whether Maudie got angry or not. At least if Hugh was found, it would be worth it, and one day Maudie would understand and forgive. Still, Jillian sat with her fingers firmly around the steering wheel, not getting out of the car.

"I know you're worried, but we're here to help the Honeycutts, Jillian," Savannah said when Jillian didn't move to get out of the car. "I didn't promise Maudie anything, so I'll do the talking."

Jillian smiled at her friend. "Thanks. Let's go."

Inside, Deputy Laura Lee Zane was at the reception desk, reading something on the computer screen. A quick smile lit up her face when she saw her friends arrive. "Good evening, ladies."

Savannah led the way to the front desk. "Hi, Laura Lee. Is Sheriff Henderson available?"

"He is, but I believe he's getting ready to leave." Laura Lee appeared for a moment as though she wanted to ask what had brought Savannah and Jillian to the sheriff's station on a Friday evening, but she must have decided against it. Instead, she picked up the phone and punched a button. "Sheriff, there are two ladies here to see you." She listened a few seconds, hung up, and dipped her head in the direction of his office. "Go ahead back."

Jillian and Savannah walked down the short hallway and into Coy Henderson's office, where the sheriff sat behind a metal desk.

"Hello, ladies. What can I do for you?"

"We're here about Hugh Honeycutt." Jillian curled her fingers inward as she broke her promise.

The sheriff didn't twitch an eyelash. "Okay."

"He's missing," Savannah said. "Since yesterday."

"Right." His impassive face told them nothing.

"Does that mean you know about it?" Jillian's instincts told her that he was already aware of the situation, and the tightness in her middle relaxed a little.

Sheriff Henderson blew out a breath and pointed at two chairs across from his desk. "Sit. Tell me what's on your mind."

Jillian perched on the edge of her seat. "Excuse me, Sheriff, but when did you find out about Hugh being gone?"

His chair squeaked as he settled into it. He leaned back and locked his fingers over his stomach, saying nothing.

"It's just that we thought no one knew that Hugh was gone," Savannah said. "Maudie has been so secretive, and she doesn't want folks to know."

The sheriff raised an eyebrow. "Did you forget we live in Moss Hollow? We've had six, maybe seven calls since noon. Folks saying he's not showing up when and where he said he would, not answering his phone, and not coming to the door at home. Maudie, though, hasn't been one of them."

"Didn't anyone who got in touch with you think Maudie was missing too?" Jillian asked. When he didn't answer, she continued. "So I'm assuming you know she's here?"

"I'm heading out to Belle Haven to have a talk with her now."

The fact that Sheriff Henderson knew Maudie was at Belle Haven shouldn't have surprised Jillian, but it did. Who had told him? "Did Farris talk to you?" she asked.

"Farris?"

"Hugh's brother." Jillian found it surprising that the sheriff didn't seem to know about Farris.

"Did you know Farris's wife, Della, is missing too?" Savannah said.

Sheriff Henderson glanced up at Savannah briefly, then made another note. "Tell me what else you know."

The story spilled out of Jillian, and Savannah added specifics of their interaction with Farris. The sheriff said nothing as he listened, but he made a note from time to time.

When the women had finished sharing, he asked, "Did you get any kind of feeling there was a menace to Hugh or Della from the brother?"

"Menace?" Jillian hadn't even considered Farris being a danger to Hugh or Della. "Why would anyone want to hurt either of them?" But even as she said the words, the notion found root in her mind and bloomed quickly. She turned to Savannah. "That's not possible, is it? I mean, you don't think Farris could have . . ."

"Oh, goodness." Savannah's face lost some color. "I hadn't even considered that. I've been thinking that it was most likely Hugh just left with Della. But now that you bring it up, maybe Farris seemed so unconcerned because he knows exactly where Hugh and Della are." She turned her uneasy gaze to Jillian.

"Oh dear." Jillian swallowed hard. Why hadn't she considered this possibility before now?

"You say this fellow is still at the Honeycutts' house?" Henderson asked.

"He is." *Wait, did I say Farris was there?* Jillian thought, not for the first time, that the sheriff knew far more about the situation than he was letting on.

The sheriff sniffed. "What about Wanda Jean?"

Jillian's brow furrowed. "What about her?"

"When you were telling me all this a minute ago, you said she was upset with Maudie."

Jillian startled. "Sheriff, you can't possibly think Wanda Jean Maplewood had any hand in Hugh and Della's disappearance."

"I can't?"

Jillian shook her head. "Why would she? How could she? It's impossible."

"Of course it is," Savannah said. "Wanda Jean's feelings were bruised, and she might have been offended or even miffed, but there is no way she'd do anything to hurt Maudie."

Sheriff Henderson cocked an eye at Savannah. "And you base your opinion on what?"

"On knowing Wanda Jean all my life." Savannah sat forward in her chair. "Sheriff Henderson, you know as well as we do that she and Maudie have been inseparable for years. Besides, Wanda Jean isn't exactly young and spry. It's pretty unlikely she'd harm anyone."

The sheriff tapped his pen on the notepad. "What else?"

"What else what?" Jillian asked.

"What else are you here to ask or say?"

"We've told you everything we know," Savannah said. "I don't believe we've left anything out, have we, Jillian?"

"Not that I can think of. Oh, but I should give you these phone numbers." Jillian reached into the pocket of her jeans and pulled out the small white card Farris had given her. "These are the phone numbers for Hugh's cousins," she said as she passed it to the sheriff, "and the number on the back is for Della, Farris's wife."

He squinted at the card.

"I'll need that back, please," Jillian said.

He lifted one brow, then wrote the numbers on his notepad before returning the card to her. "Did you talk to these people?"

"Just at the party," Jillian said. "And just for a minute."

Henderson stared at her as if trying to extract her deepest secrets. "I know you, Jillian. You have good instincts and you're good at putting puzzle pieces together."

The compliment surprised her into silence.

"Do you have any more information or ideas you want to share with me?" he asked.

Jillian shook her head. "Not that I can think of. We just felt you needed to be aware that Hugh is gone, and we're worried about him. Sheriff Henderson, do you think he might be—"

The man stood and clapped his hat on his graying head. "It's been a long day. I'll walk you out."

And with that, Jillian knew they'd gleaned as much from the conversation with Coy Henderson as possible, which was as close to nothing as they could have gotten. Laura Lee watched with considerable curiosity as the three of them left the building.

"Good night," Henderson tipped his hat slightly when they reached Jillian's car, then made his way to his cruiser.

"How do you like that?" Jillian muttered as they got in.

"If nothing else," Savannah said, "I'm glad he's aware of what's going on. But I wish he'd told us a little something."

Jillian scoffed. "A little something. When he says anything, you can bank on it being only 'a little something.' I wonder what he's going to do now."

"He said he was going to Belle Haven, but did you notice how his ears pricked forward when we mentioned Farris?"

"I sure did. Makes me wonder if he knows something we don't. Do you suppose he's going over to Maudie's house too?"

"I do," Savannah said firmly. She slid a glance at Jillian. "You know, Maudie's house is on the way to mine."

"Why, we'd drive right past the Honeycutts' if we were heading to your place." *And we'd see if the sheriff is making a pit stop there to visit Farris.*

"I'm suddenly very thirsty for the lemonade I made earlier."

"Let's go, then." Before she put the car in gear, Jillian picked up her phone. "Do you mind if Hunter comes over too? I told him I'd call him after we talked to Farris, and that was ages ago."

"Sure thing. Tell him to come on over."

After a quick call to Hunter to let him know the plan—minus the part about spying on the sheriff—Jillian set out for James and Savannah's house. A few minutes later, they drove past the Honeycutts' house.

"The sheriff is there." Savannah gestured toward the cruiser in the driveway. "Uh-oh. He's still in the car. Do you think he sees us?" She scrunched down in her seat as if they were in the getaway vehicle for a bank robbery.

"Are you kidding?" Jillian picked up just enough speed not to break the limit but to get past the bungalow quickly. "That man misses nothing. You can sit up now, you chicken."

Savannah straightened in the passenger seat. "Name-calling is unbecoming."

"Yes, Bertie," Jillian said with an eye roll. "Speaking of whom, we should probably call Belle Haven and let them know the sheriff will be showing up."

"He won't like it, but I agree with you. No one wants law enforcement showing up on their doorstep unexpectedly. Maudie might think he's there with bad news about Hugh."

Jillian winced. "I hadn't thought of that, but you're right. She's going to be really upset anyway."

Savannah placed the call, and by the time she was done fielding Bertie's questions, Jillian had pulled into the driveway of Savannah's trim little house. When they entered, James came to the kitchen doorway, a dish towel in his hands, his eyebrows up in surprise. A blue gingham apron with a ruffle at the hem had been clumsily tied about his middle and now hung like a limp flag at his beltline. The air from the kitchen was warm and scented with something sugary. His face was red with heat and maybe a little embarrassment.

"Hi honey," Savannah sang out. "You look adorable."

"Hey there," James said. "I didn't know we were having company. Hi Jillian."

"Hi yourself." She ran an amused gaze over him. "Nice outfit."

Savannah gave her husband a quick kiss and wiped something off his face. "How in the world did you get a streak of flour across your forehead?"

He gave her a sheepish grin and ran one hand across his balding pate. "I've been baking. Or trying to."

"You? Baking?" Jillian laughed, then got out her phone and snapped a quick picture. "I'll share this at the next Sweetie Pies meeting. Those ladies will eat it up. Pun intended."

Savannah giggled and brushed away more flour that was clinging to James's five o'clock shadow. "What have you been making? Besides a mess, I mean."

"I made Bertie's coconut layer cake," James said. "She gave me the recipe after the party. The layers are cooling on the rack. I still have to make the frosting, though."

"Hunter will be excited to hear that," Jillian said. "He's not hard to please, but I think he especially loves that cake."

"Hunter?" James asked.

"He's coming over in a few minutes," Savannah said. "He can help you frost the cake while Jillian and I drink lemonade."

"Anything for you, dear." James gave his wife a peck on the cheek.

The sound of a crash in the kitchen startled them all, and they raced into the room. Savannah put a hand to her forehead. "James, the racks!"

Jillian grimaced at the sight on the counter. Three metal cooling racks lay in a heap with smashed layers of golden cake sandwiched between them. Chunks of broken cake were scattered on the counter around the racks.

"Ugh, how did that happen?" James shook his head at the mess.

"Those collapsible racks aren't supposed to be stacked on

each other," Savannah said. "The legs aren't sturdy enough, and the metal is too slippery."

"So much for recreating Bertie's cake," James said forlornly. "Off to the garbage."

Jillian was about to offer condolences, but then she thought of Cornelia's dessert the night before. "Wait, don't toss it. You can make a trifle."

Savannah smiled. "I knew I kept you around for a reason, Jillian. Great idea."

"How are we going to do that?" James didn't look convinced.

"I've got some lime curd in the pantry, and we'll make some fresh whipped cream." Savannah started to retrieve supplies. "All we have to do is cube the cake and layer it with the other ingredients."

James had been reaching to untie his apron, but he stopped. "If you're sure."

"Of course, honey," Savannah said. "It won't be what you were trying for, but it'll still be delicious."

"While you're doing that, I'm going to make a few calls." Jillian edged toward the door.

"You can use my office," Savannah said. "Take notes. There's paper and a pen on the desk."

Jillian's first call was to Hugh's cell phone, and she prayed as she dialed that she'd hear his familiar voice greet her. But it went straight to voice mail. She left a message for him to return her call and sent a text telling him the same thing.

She pulled out the business card Farris had given her and tapped in Della's number. It rang once, and then a robotic message told her the mailbox was full. Jillian sent a quick text asking Della to get in touch, but she didn't expect much to come of it. After all, Farris had said Della rarely answered or returned calls. She wondered if Della would respond to the sheriff's call.

She chewed on her lower lip, pondering what little she knew.

Something sinister crept into her mind. Maybe there was a reason why neither Hugh nor Della had returned anyone's calls. Farris's visage floated before her mind's eye.

Suddenly she felt light-headed. She fought off dizziness, knowing if she gave in to her fears and worst imaginings, her efforts would become ineffectual. She gulped in a deep breath and pulled her spine straight, determined not to let those dark thoughts take over her common sense.

Flipping the card over, Jillian stared at the names *Sheldon and Starla Higgins*. The image of the immaculately and expensively dressed couple popped into her head. Their cool, dismissive attitude toward the guests at the anniversary party had left a bad taste in Jillian's mouth, but she swallowed it back and dialed the number listed next to Starla's name. A cultured, recorded voice answered, requesting a message.

"Hello, Mrs. Higgins. This is Jillian Green, Hugh and Maudie's friend from Moss Hollow. Could you please return my call as soon as you get this message? It's rather important. Thank you." She sent a similar text message and hoped for a response.

Three calls and no answers. Despite her best efforts and determination, her fears and desperation grew.

Her next call was to the Nathan County Hospital. She gave her name and asked for an update on Wanda Jean's condition.

"She's in serious but stable condition and resting quite comfortably," the operator said. "We're monitoring her closely, but there has been no change."

"That's all you can tell me?"

"Yes, sorry. We should know more tomorrow, Ms. Green, if you want to call back then."

"All right. Thank you."

Jillian flopped back against Savannah's desk chair, curling her fingers into fists to stop her hands from shaking. Why was it so hard to get information when you wanted it badly? She was glad that Wanda Jean was being cared for and was overjoyed that her condition hadn't worsened. But was she facing surgery? A long hospital stay? Was the heart attack severe? Debilitating?

The doorbell rang, startling her out of her thoughts.

"That'll be Hunter," she called toward the kitchen as she left the office and entered the foyer. "I'll get the door."

"Hi there." Hunter greeted her with a big smile as she opened the door. "Fancy meeting you here."

She grabbed his arm and pulled him inside, that fearsome feeling inside diminishing a little. "I'm so glad to see you," she said, giving him a tight hug.

He returned the embrace warmly, then pulled back a bit, tipping her face to meet his eyes. His smile faded. "What's wrong?"

"Nothing's wrong, exactly. I'm just frustrated." She refused to admit to her fear, even to those she loved.

"All of us are frustrated," Savannah said, coming to the kitchen door with a white mixing bowl cradled in one arm, stirring with a stainless-steel whisk in the other hand. Jillian never understood why Savannah preferred to whip cream by hand, but her friend always insisted that it just tasted better. "We can't seem to put anything together logically that will help us find Hugh or his sister-in-law."

"I'm about half-convinced they don't want to be found," James said over his wife's shoulder.

"Oh, surely you don't believe that." Savannah whipped the bowl's contents vigorously.

James shrugged. "If they ran off together, is it really so hard to believe they wouldn't want to be found?" Then he smiled at his wife. "Granted, I couldn't imagine wanting to run off with anyone else, so I can't really put myself in the shoes of someone who would."

Savannah beamed at him. "I'm glad to hear it."

Jillian slid a look at Hunter, who leaned over and whispered in her ear, "I'll never run away either. Pinkie promise."

"See that you don't," she whispered back. At a regular volume, she said, "I've been fighting the awful feeling that—"

Her cell phone rang. She grabbed it off the coffee table and glanced at the screen. "Farris is calling. I hope he has some news for us. *Good* news."

She had barely answered the call when Farris's voice boomed in her ear. "Jillian Green, how dare you!"

Jillian winced and pulled the phone from her ear while Farris continued his dressing down.

"I trusted you! I told you about Della and me and my brother in good faith, and you reward my honesty by going straight to the sheriff to accuse me of who knows what. That's what I call dirty dealing, Jillian." Even without having her phone on speaker, Jillian knew his voice was carrying clearly to the others in the room.

"I did not sic the sheriff on you, Farris," Jillian said quietly, hoping to calm him.

"Then how did he know everything I'd told only you and that friend of yours?"

"All we did was talk to him. We're trying to find Hugh and Della—"

"So you say, but I don't believe you," Farris said. "I told you Della doesn't want to be found, and I doubt my brother does either. And I didn't have a thing to do with their disappearance. You just call that lawman and tell him so. Tell him I didn't do a thing to either of them."

"I'm sorry if you feel threatened. That was never our intention. We're just trying to find your brother and your wife. Surely you can understand that."

Her only answer was a dial tone. Farris had hung up.

Savannah met Jillian's gaze. "I wonder what Sheriff Henderson said to him."

"Obviously whatever it was upset him," Jillian said. "What I wonder is what Henderson found out. You know our sheriff can get blood out of stone."

"Judging from all the hollering coming over your phone, I'd say whatever it was, it wasn't good," James said.

"Is this man likely to become aggressive or violent?" Hunter asked.

Jillian shook her head. "I don't think so."

"He doesn't seem the sort," Savannah added.

"Maybe not, but you can never tell," James said. "Hugh and Della are still missing. If Farris had anything to do with it, he's going to protect himself."

Jillian suddenly felt dizzy, and she gripped Hunter's arm to keep herself upright.

"Are you okay?" Hunter slid an arm around her waist to support her.

"Jillian, sit down before you fall down," Savannah ordered. "James, please take this bowl to the kitchen and bring her a glass of water."

While James complied, Hunter led Jillian to the sofa. She sank onto a cushion and rested her head in her hands for a few moments. Gradually, the light-headedness faded, and her strength returned. She lifted her head. "Sorry about that."

"You might be a little dehydrated or hungry," Savannah said. "We've been chasing after this dilemma all evening, and it's been hot as blazes outside. When's the last time you had something to eat or drink?"

Jillian straightened, remembering the salad she'd eaten at Belle Haven before hurrying off to talk with Farris. "I ate supper."

"Here." James handed her a glass of water.

"I'm fine," she protested.

"What good will it do you, or Maudie, or Hugh, or anyone if you get sick?" Hunter demanded. "Drink up."

Jillian obediently downed the water. "You're right. I've been too preoccupied about Hugh's disappearance, I suppose." She looked at Savannah. "Can I still take you up on that offer of lemonade from earlier?"

"You bet." Savannah hurried into the kitchen, saying over her shoulder, "And as soon as we get James's trifle put together, you're going to eat a huge helping. No arguments."

A while later, they sat in the Wilsons' small dining area with dessert and coffee.

"You two really worked some magic with this trifle," Jillian said after she took the first bite. "It literally melts in the mouth."

"Reminds me of Bertie's coconut cake, but with lime," Hunter said. The others all chuckled, leaving him to ask, "Did I miss something?"

"I about ruined dessert, but Savannah saved me," James said, beaming at his wife.

"It was a team effort." Savannah kissed her husband's cheek.

As they enjoyed the delightful dessert, however, thoughts of Hugh and Della's disappearance weren't far from Jillian's mind.

"Do you have any idea when they went missing?" James asked. Apparently Jillian wasn't the only one still brooding on it.

"Not exactly," Jillian answered. "Apparently both were gone from the house by the time their spouses got up."

"Were both cars gone?" James took a sip of coffee.

"Just Hugh's pickup," Jillian said.

"What about their clothes?"

"I asked Farris, and he didn't know if they took anything or not." Jillian sighed. "And Maudie refused to talk about nearly everything, so I don't know if Hugh's clothes are missing."

"So did Farris or Maudie hear them stirring around?" Hunter asked. "Or hear them leave, maybe?"

"Maudie won't talk," Jillian said again. "We have nothing solid to go on, no leads. Nothing."

"All we have are notions and suspicions," Savannah said glumly.

"That they went away together?" Hunter asked.

"That theory does seem to be floating to the top," Jillian said. "But I don't want to believe it, and I'm not going to believe it until it's proven."

James drained his coffee. "You know if anyone can get to the bottom of this, it's Coy Henderson."

Savannah nodded. "We know."

"And you know we're going to keep hoping and praying for the best outcome," Hunter added.

"We know that too." Jillian smiled at him and gave his hand a quick squeeze.

"I'm not working tomorrow," Hunter said, "so I'll visit some of the gas stations and convenience stores to see if anyone remembers seeing the two of them."

"I'll take the roads toward Bristow, if you want to take the ones going toward Painter's Ridge," James said.

"That's a great idea," Savannah said. "I'll go with you, honey."

"You'll need photos of them." Jillian scrolled through her phone. "I got some the other night at the party. I'll send them to your phone, Savannah."

"That'll be a big help," she said. "Thanks, Jillian."

"What about me?" Hunter asked.

"I'm going with you, of course." Jillian shot him a wink.

Savannah refilled everyone's coffee, then returned to her seat. "This evening, I witnessed a first, at least for myself: Sheriff Henderson paying a compliment."

"Oh yeah?" James helped himself to another serving of trifle. "What was it?"

"Now let me see if I can recall his exact words." Savannah adopted a gruff manner. "'Jillian, you have good instincts.'"

James whistled appreciatively. "Wow."

Hunter tapped on his phone. "I'm marking this day down on

my calendar. In fact, I believe I'll celebrate with another helping of trifle."

No one met Jillian at the front door of Belle Haven as she had expected, and she was uncertain if that was a good thing or a bad thing. The visit from Coy Henderson had surely caused a stir, but maybe it had dissolved Maudie's resistance to finding Hugh. Spotting a light spilling from the living room, Jillian knew that she might soon have her answer.

She walked into the room and was met by three pairs of human eyes. The dogs were nowhere to be seen. "Good evening," she said in greeting. "Why aren't you ladies in bed? It's late."

Maudie folded her arms across her chest and her expression turned even stonier. She ran her gaze over Jillian as if appraising her value. "It's amazing to me how you can just stand there, all calm and cool, when you've broken your word and deceived your friend."

Jillian held up one hand in a placating gesture. "Now, Maudie, I didn't—"

"You promised me." Maudie leaned forward, eyes glittering. "'All right, Maudie. I promise,' you said. 'Don't worry about anything right now.' That's what you told me, missy. Looked me right straight in the eye and said it."

"I didn't—"

"You did! I told all y'all I did not want my private business all over town, but what do you reckon? It's all over town, anyway. And who do I blame for that? Not Wanda Jean Maplewood, my best friend in the world who I found out this very evening now lies at death's door in the hospital. Never you even mind that I can't go see her because that hospital won't let me. No, I blame *you*, Jillian Green!"

Jillian gestured for Maudie to calm down. "But if you'll just listen to me, you'll understand—"

"I will *not* listen to you!" Maudie slapped her palm down on the arm of the chair. Possum, who was resting nearby on Cornelia's lap, leaped up and ran out of the room. "I do not want you to speak to me again until or unless I tell you to do so. With your family as my witnesses, I declare it!"

Jillian looked helplessly at Bertie and Cornelia. "Can't you make her understand that it was never my intention to hurt or betray her? All I'm trying to do is find Hugh and Della—"

Maudie jumped to her feet so suddenly she nearly toppled over. Jillian grabbed her arm to steady her and was rewarded by an icy glare as Maudie yanked free of her grasp.

"I don't want to hear those names!" Without another word, Maudie stormed out of the room and up the stairs.

"Jillian, forevermore," Bertie said in what could only be described as a growl. "What were you thinking, sending the sheriff to the house?"

"I didn't send him," Jillian protested.

Cornelia scoffed. "So he was just hankering to see us and decided to come out here for a social call?"

"I had *nothing* to do with his call, social or otherwise. He was getting ready to come to Belle Haven before we saw him. In fact, we caught him just before he left."

The twins gave her identical frowns.

"Excuse me?" Bertie said.

"Time to spill, young lady." Cornelia pointed to the seat Maudie had just vacated.

Jillian sat down. "Savannah and I went to see Farris, just like I told you we were going to do. After we talked to him, we thought we should go to the sheriff."

"So Farris told you something important, did he?" Bertie asked, her frown dissolving into curiosity.

"It's not so much what he said, but how he acted," Jillian answered. "He seemed so indifferent. As if Hugh and Della's absence didn't bother him in the least."

"I don't understand that," Cornelia said. "If my Raymond had ever—"

"Hush, Sister." Bertie made a shushing motion. "Let her finish. Go on, Jillian."

"Farris seemed far more interested in Maudie's well-being than in his wife's or his brother's. There's a backstory to it all that no one in Moss Hollow knows about. Apparently not even Wanda Jean."

"My stars," Bertie murmured.

Jillian nodded. "In the same way none of us knew Hugh had a brother, we've never known about his younger years."

"My goodness, child, tell us." Cornelia edged forward on her seat.

As succinctly as possible, Jillian related her and Savannah's conversation with Farris and the observations the friends had made based on the discussion. "By the time we got to the car, we were both convinced Sheriff Henderson needed to talk to Farris. We figured he could get more information than we could." Jillian looked at Bertie. "Did Maudie at least file a missing person's report?"

Bertie shook her head. "She firmly believes he ran off with his sister-in-law, and she has convinced our sheriff that's what happened."

"But he wouldn't! Not Hugh." No matter how many times Jillian heard the theory, she still couldn't stomach it.

"This is all quite interesting," Cornelia said, "but are you sure you did not ask Coy to come out here?"

Bertie frowned at her sister. "Cornelia, Jillian is about as good a liar as you are a horse jockey. If she says she didn't ask him to come to Belle Haven, then she didn't do it."

Cornelia folded her hands in her lap and gave Bertie a level gaze. "Don't you get in a snit. I'm just double-checking." She turned to Jillian. "Of course I believe you, honey. You aren't the kind to stir up trouble on purpose. And at least Savannah called to warn us he was coming. I thought we might have to sit on Maudie when we told her, but she was good about it. She saved all her anger and dished it out to you. She didn't dish as much as I thought she would, though."

"You handled it well, by the way," Bertie added.

"Did I?" Jillian slumped in her chair. "With the three of you shooting daggers out of your eyes at me, I thought about hiding in the cellar."

"Daggers? Piffle." Cornelia got to her feet. "You let your imagination get away from you sometimes, Jillian. Now, where is Possum? Raymond and I need to have a little chat about this situation."

14

At nine o'clock the next morning, Jillian set down her cookie dough scoop and glanced at the clock on the wall in The Chocolate Shoppe's kitchen. Hunter would be coming to pick her up in about an hour.

She was making five dozen chocolate chip cookies for Rock Valley Church's "Singspiration" that night. It was an annual event, held outside on the small rural church's grounds, and the music usually lasted long into the night. She couldn't help but think of Hugh and Maudie's party just a week before, and how everyone had anticipated fun, festivities, and fellowship. There had been music that evening too.

"What a difference a few days make," she murmured as she slid two large cookie sheets into the oven and closed the door. After setting a timer, she turned to Lenora, who was getting ready to carry a fresh tray of doughnuts to the display case. "I'm going to call the hospital and see how Wanda Jean's doing. Before I do, would you like me to take those out front for you?"

"Sure, honey. Thank you. I hope she's doing better this morning, bless her heart."

"I hope so too. No one has called me, so I'm going to take that as 'no news is good news.'"

Jillian added the tray of doughnuts to the dwindling supply in the case, then stripped off her gloves, pulled her phone from her pocket, and dialed the hospital. She made her request to the woman who answered, then hummed along with the hold music.

Stewie Franks came into the bakery and saluted her with the folded newspaper in his hand.

Maggie was busy with another customer, so Jillian asked, "What can I get you, Stewie?"

"Two bear claws and a black coffee, if you please. Are you talking to your sweetheart?"

She grinned at him and shook her head. "I'm calling to see how Wanda Jean is doing today."

He lost his smile. "I was sorry to hear about her. Let me know what you find out, will you?"

"I sure will."

Jillian stayed on the line while she served Stewie his breakfast. As he went to his table, the canned music stopped abruptly, and the operator came back on the line. The brief update the woman gave her left Jillian feeling dissatisfied. She frowned at her phone as she ended the call.

"Well?" Stewie prompted.

She went to his table and sat down, her back to the door. "She's a little better today. They're keeping her in the hospital and monitoring her condition. That's pretty much what they told me last night when I called, and it's all I know."

"It's not much," Stewie agreed.

"I wish I had better news to share."

"Aww, don't frown. Your face might freeze that way, and it'd be a shame if it did."

She forced a little smile. "I certainly don't want my face to freeze in a frown."

"Sure enough. Look at my mug. Eighty-three years old, it is."

"You have a nice face, Stewie. Lots of character to it."

"Mm-hmm." He sipped his coffee. "Just don't let yours get like mine if you can help it."

The bell above the door rang as someone came into the bakery. The cloying scent of heavy perfume reached them. Stewie glanced past her and dropped his coffee cup to the table with a clatter.

"Thunderation, what has that woman done to herself?" he asked, gaping.

Jillian turned to follow his gaze. She could hardly believe what she saw.

Maudie Honeycutt—her once-white hair now virtually glowing from red dye, her face slathered with makeup, and false eyelashes framing her eyes—strode across the floor toward them. Her green dress was bright enough to see from three blocks away. Her matching high heels clicked against the tile floor.

"Hello there," she said. "Put your eyes back in your head, Stewie. It's me."

He worked his mouth a couple of times before he croaked out, "I see who it is."

"Good morning, Mau—"

She gave Jillian a cold look and held up one hand, her long, pink nails gleaming in the light. "I said everything that I have to say to you last night, young woman."

Stewie scowled. "Why, Maudie, what a way to talk to Jillian."

"*You* don't know what this girl did," Maudie said, turning on him, "and I'm not going to tell you. So you mind your own business, Stewie Franks."

"I understand you're going through a hard time right now, so I'll forgive you for your appalling manners today. Excuse me. Jillian, I hope you have a nice day." Stewie stood and strode out of The Chocolate Shoppe, leaving his coffee and breakfast unconsumed and his newspaper unread.

"My goodness," Maudie said, staring after him. "What's gotten into Stewie?"

Bertie bustled across the room from the kitchen door. "Maybe the fact that you were just shockingly rude to him. I'll thank you not to chase away my customers." She crossed her arms. "And what have you let Jasmine do to you? You said you were going to the Clip & Curl for a haircut this morning."

Maudie drew herself up. "I didn't come here for a lecture from you, Bertie Harper. I decided to get more than a haircut."

"That is painfully obvious," Bertie said. "Why'd you do that?"

"Because if Hugh can go running off and start a new life, so can I."

"You're going to run off?" Jillian asked.

"Not exactly. At least, not yet. But I'm fixing to make changes." Maudie's tone turned more solemn. "Now, kindly remember I'm not talking to you."

"The first change you need to make is your outfit," Bertie said. "Why are you wearing that thing? And go wash your face before anyone sees you. There's soap and washcloths in that little cabinet in the bathroom."

"I have no intention of washing my face or changing my clothes, thank you very much." Maudie smoothed out her skirt. "Just because I'm staying at your house, it does not mean you can tell me what to do. I'm not a child."

Bertie frowned at her friend. "I know you're not. But this is not the way to handle what's going on right now, Maudie."

"Wrong. This is not the way *you* would handle things. Well, guess what? I have turned to a new page in my book." Maudie gestured to Jillian. "Your own granddaughter uprooted herself from California and started over again. I may not be as young as her, but I have some gumption."

"Jillian had a good reason to make the change and come back home," Bertie said.

Maudie's penciled-in eyebrows went up. "And I don't? You know as well as I do my husband ran off with Della. What am I supposed to do, sit around and twiddle my thumbs waiting for him to show up again?" She glowered out the window, her mouth a thin, tight line. "At least I'm not lying half-dead in the hospital like Wanda Jean."

Bertie and Jillian exchanged a glance. Bertie sat down and covered one of Maudie's hands with her own. "Look at me, Maudie," she said quietly. "Come on now."

Maudie shifted her gaze enough to meet Bertie's. "Yes?"

"You and I have known each other for a long time. You've been a regular customer of mine since The Chocolate Shoppe opened, and you've been part of the Sweetie Pies since it began. You have been there for me and my sister, and for Jillian too, whenever we've needed a friend."

"And Wanda Jean," Maudie said in a choked whisper. "She's been there for us all."

"Yes, she has," Bertie said. "And I'm so grateful."

"So am I," Jillian added.

Maudie slid a quick glance her way but said nothing.

"In the last week," Bertie continued, "your world has been turned topsy-turvy, and in the days leading up to that point, you had worked so hard putting the party together that you were exhausted before it even started. I don't believe you've had a good rest since before your anniversary." Maudie opened her mouth, but Bertie shushed her. "No, don't say anything. Let me finish. You've had very little recuperative rest, hardly anything to eat, and your mind has been in a constant state of turmoil."

Maudie nodded and lowered her head. She sniffled.

"So doesn't it make sense that you shouldn't be making any changes or doing anything drastic until everything is settled?"

Maudie lifted her head. Her eyes were red-rimmed, but dry. "You mean until Hugh divorces me?" Her voice cracked.

"No, that's not what I mean. Let's just take it easy until he's found and—"

"He doesn't want to be found!" Maudie cried.

Bertie took in a deep breath. "At least for now, until you feel better—"

"I feel fine!"

"Maudie, you don't. You're peaked, you've lost weight. You are not yourself. So let Cornelia, Jillian, and me take care of you for a while longer. And later on, if you want to make changes, then you'll make good choices."

Maudie's eyebrows rose almost to her hairline. "You're saying my red hair is not a good choice?"

This question brought Bertie's and Jillian's gazes to the bright hue.

"I love your white hair," Jillian said diplomatically. "I always have."

Bertie nodded. "And you don't need the big eyelashes."

"You're beautiful, Maudie." Jillian patted her shoulder. "You don't need to change, not a bit."

The woman's eyes filled as she turned to Jillian. "Really?"

"Absolutely."

"Then why—" She swallowed hard. She had difficulty getting the words out, but she finally said, "Why did Hugh fall for that bleached blonde with the fluffy eyelashes?"

Jillian wondered the same thing, and she had no good answer to offer. In fact, nothing about the entire situation made sense.

"Let's not think about that right now," Bertie said. "Let's just enjoy spending some time together. When I get home this afternoon, you and I will go upstairs and look at that little apartment again. If you want to fix it up and stay in it awhile, then we'll do that."

Maudie's posture seemed to lighten. "You wouldn't mind?"

"Not a bit. You're good company for Cornelia during the day, and for Jillian and me when we get home."

Again Maudie cast a sideways glance to Jillian. "Cornelia said you didn't send the sheriff out to the house."

"No, I didn't."

"You promise?"

"One hundred percent promise I did not send the sheriff to see you."

"Okay, then." Maudie sniffled. "I'm not mad at you."

"That is truly a relief," Jillian said with a genuine smile. Out of the corner of her eye, she spotted Hunter's car pulling up in front of the bakery. She hurriedly got out of her seat. "I have to go now. I'll see you both later."

Jillian removed her apron and hairnet, then washed her hands. She grabbed several cookies out of the display case and put them in a bag. Hunter walked in with a wave, then waited for her by the counter.

"Ready?" she asked.

"I am." He sent a curious gaze toward the corner. "Who is that woman with the bright red hair talking so intently with Bertie?"

"I'll tell you in the car."

A few moments later, they were settled in the car with the air conditioner on full blast. Despite only being midmorning, the day's heat and humidity were already skyrocketing.

"Okay, we're in the car," Hunter said, "so tell me."

"When I got home last night, Maudie was fit to be tied, thinking I had told Coy Henderson to go out and talk to her. She declared she'd never speak to me again, then stormed off upstairs. I'm not sure what happened between then and now to make her suddenly decide she needed an extreme makeover, but she did. You just saw the results."

"That was Maudie?" Hunter sounded as incredulous as Jillian expected. "It was certainly different."

"Just be glad you weren't there when she hollered at Stewie and he left in a snit."

His mouth flew open. "I'm sorry, what? Who could yell at him?"

"Apparently Maudie can if she's worked up enough."

"I don't understand. Why would she do that?"

"Because she is firmly convinced that Hugh has left her for Della."

"So instead of trying to locate him and find out what's going on . . ." Hunter's voice trailed off.

"Right. But I think Bertie is getting through to her."

"I hope so. I can't imagine what these last few days have been like for her, but I know it's been tough."

"If only there was something definite that we knew. Having nothing but guesses and speculations isn't cutting it."

"Maybe we'll find someone who saw them buying gas at one of the stations in the area. Or perhaps the sheriff will turn up something."

"Here's hoping." Jillian crossed her fingers. "We'd better get started on our quest and not waste any more time."

Jillian's cell phone rang just as Hunter pulled out of his parking spot. She looked at the screen and felt a flutter of nervous energy. "It's Hugh's cousin Starla. I left a message for her last night." She pressed the talk button and put the phone to her ear. "Hello, Starla. Thank you so much for calling back."

"Good morning," Starla said in her cool, professional voice. "I apologize for not getting in touch with you sooner, but as I told your sheriff a few minutes ago, Sheldon and I have been terribly busy, and I hadn't even checked my phone for texts or messages. I'm just now going through them while we're waiting to board our flight. I assume you're calling about Hugh and Della. What's going on? The sheriff told us next to nothing, which I found maddening to the extreme. Answering questions with questions is one of my biggest pet peeves."

"Sheriff Henderson isn't typically one to be forthcoming with details," Jillian said. "And yes, I did call about Hugh and Della. They haven't been seen in a couple days. I was hoping you'd talked to one or both of them, or that you might know where they could be."

"They're missing?"

"Since Thursday morning, or maybe Wednesday night."

"Oh, my. This is distressing news. How is Maudie? She's not gone too, is she?"

Jillian paused before answering. "She's staying with me. She's doing as well as can be expected, under the circumstances." *Considering everything, this isn't actually a lie.* "Starla, have you or your husband heard from either of them?"

"No, but we've never been in close contact with either of them, so that isn't surprising or significant. Where do you think they are? What do you think happened?"

"Actually, we're at a loss. I was hoping maybe you could give us a little insight."

"Insight?"

"Do you think—that is, is it possible that Hugh and Della might have left together?"

There was a heavy pause before Starla answered. "Anything is possible, but I hardly think it's likely. I haven't been around Hugh much in recent years, but he isn't the type to do something as ridiculous as running off with someone else."

Jillian frowned, comparing Starla's words to what Farris had said the night before. "What about Della?"

There was a brief silence. "Della is another matter. She's a flake. Always has been, and it seems to me the years haven't changed her a bit."

"Oh?"

"You saw her at the party, didn't you? Acting as if she didn't have a brain, whooping and singing, being foolish and making a spectacle of herself. Of course, she's married to Farris, so what can one expect?"

Jillian grew still. "What do you mean?"

"Why, he's as flaky as his wife." Starla made the declaration as though it shouldn't be a surprise to Jillian. "The way they turned into a couple of vagrants, drifting from state to state, never settling in one place long enough to put down any kind of roots. There was no reason for it. They were educated. They could have gotten real jobs somewhere."

"I thought they had a place in Sheridan."

"They do now. They're too old to ramble all over the country. They have a little one-bedroom apartment in a senior housing neighborhood, and not a penny to their names except their social security checks."

"It's not a ranch?" Jillian was sure Farris had said they had a ranch.

"Certainly not," Starla said. "How they were able to afford the trip to Georgia is anybody's guess. If you were to ask me, I'd guess Maudie paid their airfare, the hotel bill, and their car rental."

Jillian took in all this information, hoping to parse these new details for anything that might help locate the two. "Did you tell this to Sheriff Henderson?"

"I told him I hadn't seen or talked to either of them and that I have no idea where they could be."

"Is that all? Didn't he ask you about anything else?"

"Sure he did, but I had no answers. I mean, I don't know if Hugh and Della were secretly in contact all these years, or if they'd all had some kind of fight or anyone made any threats or phone calls to them. How would I know any of that?"

"I'm sure he was just asking to cover his bases," Jillian said. "We're all just trying to find Hugh and Della."

After a brief silence, Starla asked, "You aren't one of his deputies, are you?"

It was all Jillian could do not to snort into the phone. Her?

A deputy for Coy Henderson? The idea was both laughable and frightening at the same time. "No ma'am," she said, smiling a little. "I enjoy my career as a baker too much." And she much preferred to keep her amateur detective work out of view of the Nathan County sheriff's watchful eye. "Starla, I understand Della and Hugh were once engaged. Is that right?"

"Yes. Can you believe it?" Starla gave a brief, rather humorless laugh. "Thank goodness that knot never got tied."

"Do you think there might still be romantic feelings between them?"

"I seriously doubt Hugh would have any such feelings toward Della, but I wouldn't put anything past her. Again, I refer to her antics Saturday night. Didn't you notice?"

"Yes, I did. So do you think Farris could have gotten jealous?"

"Perhaps. But if you're asking because you believe he might have given in to a fit of jealous rage and caused trouble, I'd say it's unlikely. Farris has always lacked spunk and motivation. Hold, please." After a few moments, Starla came back on the line. "They're announcing our flight, so I have to go. I hope I've helped you, at least a little."

"Thank you for taking the time to talk to me."

"Please get in touch the minute you hear anything, would you?"

Jillian agreed and wished Starla a safe flight, then disconnected the call. By this time, Hunter and Jillian had passed the city limits and were on the road to Painter's Ridge.

Realizing they'd be passing the Nathan County Hospital soon, Jillian asked, "Would you mind if we stop by the hospital? After the conversation with Maudie this morning, I'd like to try to see Wanda Jean, or at least get a message to her. Both women would benefit greatly by patching up this quarrel."

"Of course," Hunter said. "I hope Wanda Jean is better by now."

"I talked with a nurse earlier, but she told me very little other than that they were continuing to keep a close eye on her. That's all I've been able to get out of them."

Hunter nodded toward the phone Jillian still held. "What did Starla have to say?"

"She gave a bit of a different spin on things. I doubt it has any bearing on this situation, though, other than to underscore that Della is a peculiar sort and Hugh is a solid, good man."

"Which we already know," Hunter said.

"Her take on Farris doesn't match up to what he told Savannah and me last night."

"In what way?"

"From what he shared with us yesterday, I got the idea he was a hardworking but underappreciated fellow, not understood by most."

"And now you think differently?"

"Maybe."

Hunter lifted one eyebrow. "What does that mean?"

"In spite of what he told us, I sensed an underlying something about him. I don't know what exactly. There was just something that he wasn't telling us."

"Do you think he had a hand in whatever's happened to his brother and his wife?"

Jillian stared out her window at the sunbaked landscape. "I think it's possible. I hope and pray Hugh is all right, but I am getting really worried."

The brunette nurse behind the desk glanced up as Jillian and Hunter approached her. "May I help you?"

"I'm Jillian Green, and I'm checking about Wanda Jean Maplewood."

"I believe I talked with you earlier this morning."

Jillian gave her a brief smile. "Your voice does sound familiar."

The nurse turned to the computer monitor on the desk and clicked the mouse a few times. After a moment, she said, "There's nothing more to tell you at this time."

"I'd like to talk with her, please."

"I'm sorry, but still no visitors."

"Is that doctor's orders or her own request?"

The nurse straightened in her desk chair as if preparing for a battle of wills. "It's Mrs. Maplewood's wishes."

Jillian took a pen and a small notebook from her purse and wrote a quick note, which she tore out, folded in half and held out to the nurse. "Would you please take this to her and wait for a reply?"

The nurse hesitated, then took the note. "Excuse me." She moved swiftly from behind the desk and went down the corridor, where she opened the third door on the left.

Hunter rested one hand on Jillian's shoulder. His touch gave her such comfort that she leaned against him briefly, hoping to absorb some of his calm strength.

"Please don't worry," he said.

"It's hard not to worry when everything seems so cloudy and nothing makes sense."

"I know, but we'll just keep pressing on. James and Savannah are doing their best too. And the sheriff has never dropped the ball. I'm sure he's not about to start."

"Even if there is no official investigation?"

"Even then."

She closed her eyes and prayed he was right.

"Here she comes," Hunter said quietly, and Jillian opened her eyes.

The nurse took her place behind the desk. "You may go in. Room 214." She pointed a pencil toward it.

"Thank you." Jillian grabbed Hunter's hand and hurried to Wanda Jean's room, hoping her friend didn't change her mind before they got to her. The door was ajar, and she knocked gently. "Wanda Jean? It's Jillian."

She poked her head inside and was surprised to see the woman sitting in a chair by the window. Her thick, wavy, silver-streaked hair hung loose past her shoulders. Other than being slightly pale and having an IV attached to her arm, she appeared as healthy as ever. Wanda Jean smiled and waved Jillian into the room.

"Hunter is with me," Jillian said. "Is it okay to bring him in here?"

"Sure. Have him come in."

They entered the room with its single bed and assortment of cards and flowers. Wanda Jean stretched out one hand, and Jillian took it briefly, noting how chilly her fingers felt.

"Would you like me to get you a blanket?" Jillian asked.

"No." Wanda Jean shook her head. "I'm fine, thank you."

"You're looking good, Wanda Jean," Hunter said.

Her smile was warm and grateful. "I feel good, and I think I'm going home in a day or two."

Jillian frowned. "Really? But every time I've called—"

Wanda Jean let go of Jillian's hand and waved dismissively. "They told you there's been no change, right? That's because I asked them to say that. Sit down." She pointed to the bed.

Jillian perched on the edge of the bed. "Why would you do that? Everyone is so worried about you."

"Honey, I've been sick," Wanda Jean said. "Sick at heart, physically and emotionally. I needed time to think, to reevaluate my life and my spirit. I couldn't do that with folks coming in here, talking to me. It's bad enough with nurses barging in, poking at me, checking everything but the split ends of my hair."

"But don't you realize how concerned folks have been for you?"

Wanda Jean ducked her head in what Jillian defined as embarrassment. "I know what people say about me," she murmured. "I'm sure they thought me being in here with my mouth shut was the best thing that could have happened."

"Wanda Jean, I—"

"Hush." Wanda Jean looked from Jillian to Hunter. "I know I'm the town gossip. I gather and pass out rumors like they're baseball cards. And when I really think about it, I'm ashamed of myself."

Time without visitors really has given her some perspective, Jillian thought. Maybe it was good that Wanda Jean had been alone for a while.

Wanda Jean cleared her throat. "So I have decided to turn over a new leaf. Or try, anyway."

Jillian smiled at her. "That's wonderful, Wanda Jean. You'll feel a lot better for it, I'm sure."

"It's the right thing to do, and if it took a heart attack to help me see that, then so be it. Now I need to know: Is Maudie still mad at me?" Wanda Jean's voice broke, and the expression in her eyes pierced Jillian's heart.

Jillian scooted forward and took Wanda Jean's hand in hers. "Maudie is extremely worried about you and wants to see you. The best thing you can do for her is to let her come visit, whether here or at home."

Tears slid down Wanda Jean's pale cheeks. "Really? But she doesn't seem to want anything to do with me, and I don't understand why. It seems to be more than just my big mouth." She swallowed hard.

Jillian spoke very softly. "Actually, there's been a problem."

Wanda Jean froze, staring at her. "What kind of problem? Is Maudie okay?"

Jillian glanced at Hunter, who had been standing discreetly off to the side. After he gave her an encouraging nod, she said, "It seems Hugh has gone missing."

Wanda Jean took in a sharp breath and her fingers tightened around Jillian's. "What do you mean?"

"We don't know where he is."

Wanda Jean stared at her for what seemed like an eternity, then transferred her stunned gaze to Hunter as if pleading for a denial. "When did this happen?"

"We think Thursday morning, maybe Wednesday night," he said. "No one has seen him since then."

"I saw him."

Jillian's eyebrows shot up. "Say what? When?"

"Thursday morning, early."

"Where? And what time?"

"I have a little trouble sleeping sometimes," Wanda Jean said. "If I get up and do something, like take a drive or a walk, it helps. Thursday morning, about six thirty or so, I went to the grocery store, and there he was with that silly little woman who married his brother. Shocked me to my toes, I tell you. Why were they at Food for Less at that time of day? No one goes shopping that early, unless they can't sleep, or they're going fishing, or something like that."

"Della was with him?" Hunter asked. "You're sure?"

"Sure as the nose on your handsome face. I started to go to

them, but they paid and left before I could. And why was Hugh there with Della instead of Maudie? I wanted to ask Maudie about that. I thought maybe she was sick or something. Or maybe they were going somewhere and needed to get an early start. But she wouldn't return my calls. Leaving a text message about something like that just seemed tacky to me, so I didn't." Wanda Jean stopped speaking abruptly, her eyes going big. "Oh, my goodness. You don't think—that is . . . is Della missing too?"

Jillian nodded.

"Coy Henderson knows about this, right?" Wanda Jean asked. "Please tell me he and Laura Lee and Gooder and everybody are looking for Hugh."

"He's on the case," Jillian said. "It's possible he'll want to talk to you, so let the nurse know it's okay. Just tell him what you told us."

"Anything to help," Wanda Jean said. "I bet poor Maudie is worried sick." She pursed her lips, thinking. "I wonder. Do you think they went to the cabin?"

Jillian gaped at her. "What cabin?"

"That cabin they own down on Orchard Creek. I've been there once or twice. It was a rustic little shack they bought years and years ago. Hugh fixed it up and surprised Maudie with it. It was back in the woods, but you could see it from the road. Maudie's not one for roughing it, so they didn't use it very often. I doubt anyone has been there for a long time."

"Orchard Creek stretches for several miles," Hunter said. "Do you remember where the cabin is?"

"You really think they might be at the cabin?" Wanda Jean stiffened in her seat. "Do you think Hugh went there to get away from his brother? Or that he sneaked off there with Della? You know, I didn't trust that woman the minute I laid eyes on her, the way she threw herself on poor Hugh. Of course, he could have resisted her charms. If you ask me, he didn't try very hard."

She stopped speaking abruptly and pressed her lips together in a thin tight line. Wanda Jean may have had an epiphany of sorts while laid up in the hospital, but changing the habits of a lifetime could take her a while.

"When you see Maudie, it might be better not to say any of that to her," Jillian said gently.

Wanda Jean nodded quickly as though eager to please. "You're right, dear. I am truly going to work on watching what I say. However"—she lifted one finger to make a point—"that doesn't mean I won't still be curious about what's going on in town. I'll keep my ear to the ground, so to speak, but just to make sure nothing untoward is happening around here."

Jillian gave her a warm smile. "That's a good goal to set for yourself. But before you firmly clamp down on your resolve, is there anything else you can tell me that might help us find Hugh?"

Wanda Jean seemed to seriously contemplate Jillian's question, but she finally shook her head. "Honestly, Hugh is such a good man. He'd never leave Maudie, not for anything. And that silly Della, from what I saw, didn't have the sense to persuade him to leave, even if he was so inclined."

"What about Farris?" Jillian asked.

Wanda Jean narrowed her eyes and her hands curled into fists. "That man. He was so rude I can hardly believe he's related to Hugh."

"Go on, please." Jillian felt a sharp pang for urging the woman to spill more dirt against her resolution. She vowed to give Wanda Jean all the encouragement and support she could to help her along the way—but only after Hugh had been found and the situation settled. Wanda Jean might still have a gold mine of knowledge. And was it really gossiping when they were trying to find two missing people?

"I went over there to see Maudie that day, and Farris pitched a hissy fit like you wouldn't believe." Wanda Jean released a huffy breath. "He startled me so bad, I dropped my coffee mug on the kitchen floor. It was the mug I use every day when I'm over there. He yelled at me for coming into the house without knocking, for making coffee, and for helping myself to it. How could I have known he was in the shower when I got there? Maudie and I never knock on each other's doors. We always just walk right in. You know that."

Jillian nodded. "You've been good friends for a long time."

"We certainly have. And some skinny old man from Wyoming can't throw me out of my best friend's house. When he told me Maudie wasn't there, I left of my own accord. But I wanted to find out why she was avoiding me, so I went back."

"More than once."

"Yes. Four or five times. And kept calling. And then that last time—well, I felt like someone had kicked me in the chest, and here I am. But I'm feeling better now. They've taken good care of me."

"We're mighty glad of that," Hunter said.

"We sure are," Jillian added.

"Thank you. I know I haven't been on everyone's list of favorite people, but that's okay. Things will change." Wanda Jean switched her gaze between them a couple of times. "But after what you've told me about Hugh, I'm convinced something has happened to him. Something unplanned, like an accident somewhere. I bet Coy, or one of his men, finds his pickup upside down in a ditch or in the trees where he went off the road." Her eyes filled. "Oh Jillian. What if Hugh's dead?"

Back in the Lexus, Jillian called Sheriff Henderson. Her conversation with him was short and to the point, ending with him saying, "All right then," and disconnecting the call.

"If words cost money, Coy Henderson would be a rich man," Jillian said. "He hoards them like gold."

Hunter laughed. "At least you updated him."

"And now it's up to him what to do with the information."

"Should we continue with our plan to ask at gas stations?"

"I think we need to go to Orchard Creek and look for that cabin," Jillian said. "We can stop at any gas stations along the way."

"Sounds like a plan." Hunter hesitated before putting the car in drive. "What's the best way to get to Orchard Creek from here?"

Jillian pulled up an area map on her phone and zoomed in on the location of the creek. "You'll want to take Highway 33 to Hawk Lake Road." She leaned toward Hunter so he could see the screen. "The headwaters are in Howard County, and Orchard Creek meanders down until it peters out at Hawk Lake, a really small lake near Painter's Ridge. We can start at the bottom and work our way up. That's about twelve miles, if not more. And most of it runs along the old back roads, so it will seem longer."

Hunter studied the map. "Then we'd better get going."

They stopped at every convenience store along the way and showed photos of Hugh and Della to the clerks. None of them recalled seeing either one.

After striking out for the third time, Jillian made a face as she buckled her seat belt. "If Gooder were here right now, he'd tell me to stick to baking cookies and let Sheriff Henderson do the detective work. I'm starting to think he'd be right."

Hunter chuckled. "Nonsense. Who'd take your place looking under rocks? Wanda Jean?"

She folded her arms across her chest. "Hardly. You heard her. Turning over my sleuthing to her would compromise her resolve."

He laughed again. "You love digging up secrets and you know it, Jillian Green."

"You're right. But dead ends sure are maddening, and this business with Hugh's disappearance has been nothing but dead ends."

"Not exactly," he said. "I think your idea to find the cabin is a good one. They have to be somewhere."

"Sure they do. Like Mexico. Or California. Or Timbuktu, for all we know. Searching for this cabin is probably just a wild-goose chase."

"Maybe, maybe not. But it's the best lead we have."

"I know." She fought off the feeling of futility. The last thing Jillian wanted to do was give up. After driving in silence and watching the scenery for a few minutes, she realized something. "You know, I haven't seen any spots where an accident may have happened. If they aren't hiding out in this cabin, then I don't know what to do next. No one has seen them, except Wanda Jean. Neither one responds to calls or texts." She shuddered. "Right now, my biggest hope is that we find them safe and sound at the cabin, even if it means broken hearts."

"Hopefully the sheriff has had more success than us," Hunter said. "He has manpower and other resources that we don't."

Jillian fought back tears as she continued to stare out the window. There were few times in her life that she had felt as helpless she did right then.

They passed a sign that read *Hawk Lake Road, 1 mile.* The landscape was thick with pine trees and oaks, and the shade grew denser when they turned down a rutted dirt lane. They drove slowly for a few minutes, then the road forked when they reached the small lake.

"Which way do we go?" Hunter asked.

"Turn right," Jillian said. "We'll follow the creek's path upstream and watch for a small cabin. Keep an eye out for Hugh's pickup too."

"If no one has been to that cabin for a long time, as Wanda Jean said, then it might be falling apart by now. And she said you could see it from the road *if* you were looking for it. I figure that means it blends in so well with the landscape that you might not see it unless you knew it was there."

"If Hugh built it, it would still be standing." Jillian scanned the scenery outside her window as Hunter made the turn. "Everyone says when Hugh builds something, it will last. Do you know he was called down to Savannah to build a home for Sherman Castile?"

Hunter's eyebrows went up. "Sherman Castile, the writer?"

"That's the one. It was back in about 1992 or so. The man wanted something between an antebellum mansion and a Frank Lloyd Wright–style house."

"That sounds rather unusual."

"Hugh got with the architect, and they built it. Unusual but gorgeous. There were articles about it in all the big magazines."

"I'm impressed."

"He's retired now, but I believe he still does consulting sometimes." Worry gripped her. "He has to be all right, Hunter." Her voice cracked. "He has to be."

Hunter reached over to squeeze her hand, but he put his hand back on the steering wheel as they were jostled by another bump. They jounced along the rough road, dodging potholes and washboard ruts. Their slow speed gave them plenty of time to peer into the woods, squint past overgrown brush and scrub, and visually scour spots where the hillsides dropped.

At one point, Jillian glanced at the clock on the dashboard. Two hours had passed since Hunter had picked her up at the bakery. She closed her eyes, praying hard for guidance, strength, and a restoration of peace.

"Look!" Hunter's voice jarred her back to the present. "Through the trees there. Isn't that Hugh's pickup?" He slowed even more, and they both leaned forward, peering hard at the flash of red several yards off the road.

"Yes!" Jillian nearly whooped with excitement. "I recognize that bright-green tennis ball on his radio antenna. Maudie complained his truck was identical to a thousand others and it was hard to spot in a parking lot, so he put it on there."

Hunter eased his car forward until they saw the path the pickup had taken through the brush and trees. "It's almost as if someone tried to hide it," he muttered.

"Do you think Hugh hid it there?" She swallowed hard as a chill swept through her. "Do you think he might be in it?"

"I don't know. Wait here and I'll go see."

"Not on your life. I'm coming with you." Jillian scrambled to unfasten her seat belt and get out of the car.

Hunter moved fast on his long legs, but she kept up with him. They reached the truck at the same time. The bed was empty, swept clean as Hugh had always kept it. There wasn't a speck of trash or dirt in the cab and no signs that anyone had been in it recently. The windows were up and the doors were locked.

Jillian looked around at the thick woods and tangled undergrowth. "We haven't seen another house on this road yet, Hunter. Not a shed or a barn or mobile home."

He perused their surroundings as well. "If anyone did live around here, it was a long time ago." His gaze went to the ground and he pointed at the tracks left by Hugh's pickup. "There's no driveway here, and I doubt there ever has been. The truck was parked as far away from the road as possible. We might not have seen it, except for the color."

"I'm calling Sheriff Henderson. I'm sure we're out of Howard County now and back in Nathan." She frowned at her phone, tapping it. "Ugh, no signal. Hunter, try yours."

He pulled out his cell phone but had the same result. "We're too far out in the middle of nowhere."

"I find it extremely unlikely that Hugh's pickup just happens to be parked on a road where no one else lives but where he owns property, rustic or otherwise."

"He parked it here himself." Hunter's voice was grim.

"Exactly."

The concern and warm sympathy she'd felt toward the man she'd known all her life suddenly twisted and began to morph into something foreign—something she didn't like. It churned inside her like bile. She was suddenly certain that Della was with him, and they were hiding from the world, just as Maudie had said. Just as Farris had said. Try as Jillian might to calm the sense of betrayal and the accompanying fury, her emotions continued to rise.

"They must have parked here to hide the truck, then walked to the cabin," Hunter mused. "Neither of them is young, and they probably aren't up to trudging very far, especially in this heat. That means the cabin is likely to be nearby."

They stepped a few feet away from the pickup and once again studied their surroundings, scrutinizing every detail. Something scurried across the ground nearby, drawing Jillian's attention. It was nothing but a couple of squirrels chasing each other, but as her gaze followed their playful path, she caught sight of something down the hill.

"What's that?" She pointed.

Hunter stared hard. "I think it's a roof."

"That's what I thought."

"It's small, like maybe a chicken coop or woodshed. Maybe an outhouse."

"I bet the cabin is down there." She pulled on his sleeve. "Let's go see. If Hugh's there, which I hope and pray he is, he's got a lot of explaining to do."

The wooded hill sloped downward, away from them. Old leaves and other detritus covered most of the ground, hiding rocks, holes, or any other obstacles that could cause them to trip. Hunter and Jillian made their way downhill as quickly and carefully as the terrain allowed. Short, scrubby briar bushes clutched at their legs. Jillian fleetingly wished she'd worn jeans instead of capris. *I'd be hot, but at least my shins wouldn't be all scratched up.*

"Wait." Hunter stopped and caught her arm. "Do you hear that?"

She halted and held her breath, listening. "Music."

He nodded. "A guitar."

"And now someone is singing."

"That's obviously a woman's voice."

"I'm sure it's Della. And I'm sure Hugh is with her. Oh, those two! How could they do this to Maudie?" Jillian started toward the cabin, but Hunter stopped her.

"Let's not storm the place."

Her hands were curled in such tight fists that her knuckles were white. "Why not? I don't think I've ever been this angry in my life." She stomped one foot.

"I know how you feel, Jillian. I feel the same way, and that is exactly why we shouldn't go down there with all pistons firing. Most people don't react well when confronted by anger and accusations."

"But—"

"Our showing up is going to catch them off guard. We'll use that to our advantage. Don't look at me that way. While they are still processing how we found them, we'll just explain that everyone is worried, and people are searching for them. They won't have time to get defensive or foolish."

Jillian crossed her arms, not quite buying Hunter's plan. "And you think by coming in softly, we can talk them into going back to Moss Hollow?"

"I believe so, yes. Especially if we emphasize everyone's concern for them."

She bit her lip and glanced down the hill, where, in addition to the small outbuilding they'd first spotted, the back of the cabin could now be seen. "I just don't understand how anyone can be cruel enough to hurt others the way those two have," she said.

"I know. And I don't understand it either. Right now, though, we've found them, and we can be thankful they haven't been killed or injured."

"Oh, I'm thankful," she snapped. "But not as thankful as Maudie will be that he's still alive so she can wring his neck. If I don't beat her to it."

"Concentrate on the gratitude part," he suggested.

"I'm trying."

"Good. Let's go on down there. Be careful."

They made their way down the hill until the ground leveled off a few yards from the cabin. A stone well with a weathered hand pump stood near the cabin. It was now apparent to them why the pickup had been parked up the hill: over the years, trees had sprouted and grown between the cabin and the road. In the thick shade of their branches, there was no space for a vehicle to be driven or parked.

The sound of guitar strumming grew louder as they approached, joining the ambient noise provided by birdsong and scampering squirrels. On the front porch, in an old straight-backed chair, Hugh sat with his eyes focused on the guitar in his hands, his fingers plucking the strings in a sweet melody. His usually neat gray hair was uncombed, and a light veneer of gray whiskers grizzled his face.

"Play that again," Della hollered from inside the cabin. "This time, give it that bluesy rhythm like I told you."

Jillian took Hunter's hand. As they neared the small porch she called out, "Hugh!"

Hugh looked up, and his eyes widened. He shook his head and made a panicked shooing gesture with one hand. "Go!" he mouthed. He shot a glance toward the door and gestured again. "Hurry!"

If he was trying to get rid of them because he didn't want to be caught, it was too late. Jillian's ire stirred again. "Don't you tell us to go, Hugh Honeycutt," she said, stalking toward him. "Everyone in Moss Hollow is worried about you, so the least you can do—"

"Get out of here," Hugh growled at her, leaning forward. He toppled over, the chair with him. The guitar went flying and landed nearby. He yelped with pain. Jillian's anger evaporated immediately. She and Hunter rushed toward him. The puppy, Roscoe, ran out of the cabin, yipping wildly.

"Stop right where you are." Della stood in the open doorway. She wore a canary yellow, floor-length caftan, and her long platinum hair hung loose around her head, as wispy as the down of a dandelion. The same could not be said for the hefty pistol in her hand.

Steady as a rock, Della aimed the pistol straight at Jillian.

Jillian froze, staring at the barrel of the gun. She raised her eyes to Della, noting the woman's high color and fiery eyes. Roscoe ran around her twice, then licked her feet, his tail wagging.

"Della, Hugh is hurt," Jillian said.

Della remained silent.

"I want to check on him," Jillian said. "Please, Della?"

The woman shot a fast glance at Hugh. "He's all right. He's not crying."

Hunter took a step toward him. "He's hurt, and I'm going to take care of him."

"I said he's all right!" Della yelled, the gun pointing at Hunter now. "Leave him alone."

"He's bleeding." Hunter gestured toward Hugh.

"Bleeding?" Della repeated as if she'd never heard the word before.

"Shoot me if you want to, but I'm taking care of him." Hunter knelt next to the motionless man and felt for a pulse at his neck.

Horrified by the turn of events, Jillian stared at Hugh, grimacing at the crimson pool forming around his head on the porch floor. For the first time, she noticed that Hugh had been bound to the chair at the ankles and waist. "Why is he tied up?" she cried.

Hunter began working out the knots, and she went to help him, Roscoe at her heels.

"Hey!" Della aimed the pistol at Jillian again, holding it with both hands as if the weight of it was too heavy for her grasp. "Unless you want to be shaking St. Peter's hand soon, young lady, you'll stay right where you are. Your boyfriend can take care of Hugh.

And you, mister, tend to Hugh but leave him tethered."

Hunter met Della's eyes steadily, and his unruffled demeanor gave Jillian a measure of confidence and comfort. "I have to untie him so I can turn him over and check on him," he said. "I can't take care of him like this."

Della narrowed her eyes as if trying to read Hunter's intentions. "Then do it, but don't try to be some kind of hero. I've got your lady in my sights."

"No heroics," he promised. He loosened and removed the nylon rope that bound Hugh to the chair. "I need something to cut these zip ties from his ankles."

"You have a pocketknife?" Della asked.

"I do."

"Get it, use it, then give it to me."

Without a word, Hunter extracted a utility knife from his pocket. There wasn't much he could do with something that small except cut the ties that bound Hugh. After he was done, he handed it to Della. He moved the chair away from Hugh and turned the older man over.

Hunter examined Hugh's head, which was covered in blood. "He may need stitches. We should get him to a doctor."

Della shook her head. "You're doing fine by yourself. Put a bandage on him."

Jillian was shocked that Della would suggest a mere bandage could help Hugh, who had a gash in his forehead at least two inches wide. *How in the world can we get him safely away from her?* If only their cell phones had picked up a signal, help would be arriving.

Della bent sideways, peering at Hugh. Jillian stiffened, wondering if she could knock the woman off-balance enough to wrest the pistol from her hand.

"Huh," Della muttered. She straightened just as Jillian moved.

"Don't be getting any funny ideas about taking this pistol away from me, missy." She ran a suspicious gaze over Jillian. "In fact, you there." She gestured toward Hunter. "Leave off taking care of Hugh and come bind up your girl. She's got a look in her eyes that I don't trust. I have plenty of zip ties. Use them."

"Now, wait a minute—" Hunter said.

"No. Get inside, both of you."

Hugh moaned.

"Hugh needs—" Hunter began.

"Forget what he needs and go inside." Della made a show of aiming the pistol more resolutely at Jillian.

"All right." Hunter got to his feet.

Della's gaze shifted between Hunter and Jillian. "Lead the way, missy. You, mister, go in after your girlfriend."

With the puppy joining her and Hunter and Della close behind, Jillian stepped into the one-room cabin. She nearly recoiled when the wall of hot, stuffy inside air hit her at the doorway. It smelled musty and faintly of old woodsmoke. Even with the door and windows open, the cabin was stifling. As her eyes adjusted to the dim interior, she saw a bed, a small table, and a tiny kitchen area with a few pots and pans.

"Sit there." Della motioned to a cane-bottom chair near the table.

Jillian sat warily, watching the woman.

"The zip ties are there on the table," Della told Hunter. "Strap her ankles to the chair just like I did Hugh, and her wrists behind her. I don't want her to budge. Then use that white rope there around her middle and knot it at the back. Nice and snug." When Hunter hesitated, she snapped, "Do it! The sooner you get her secured, the sooner you can help my partner."

Hunter met Jillian's gaze and she nodded, knowing he wouldn't hurt her. She trusted that somehow the two of them would be able to find a way out of this predicament. She just didn't know how quite yet.

"Jillian, give me your hands," he said quietly from behind her.

"Cross your wrists first, and don't flex them," Della ordered. "I know all about those tricks that will help you slip out of your restraints. I read about it online. I'm going to watch and make sure you do it right."

Hunter did as Della ordered, murmuring apologies to Jillian. "All right, I'm finished. I really need to see to Hugh."

"Go ahead," Della said. "Now that she's tied up, I can trust your girlfriend isn't going anywhere or going to cause any trouble. But don't get smart and think you can pull something. I'm still gonna watch you, and I can still put a bullet in her."

They went outside. From Jillian's place within the cabin, her view of the activity on the porch was restricted. She was able to catch shadowy movements, and she heard their voices through the open door and windows. When Hugh spoke, a wave of relief hit her so hard she sagged in the chair.

"Put him on the bed," Della said as Hunter half-carried, half-dragged Hugh inside. She still had the pistol in her grip. The older man's face was covered in blood that streamed from the wound on his forehead. "If he makes any move, we're tying him up again."

She directed Hunter to a jug of water on the small table, then to the first aid kit.

"Lucky that I have a first aid kit with me all the time, huh?" she said conversationally. "I don't go anywhere without one. You never know when you'll need it." She peered at Hugh's face again. "Do a good job on that cut when you clean it. It doesn't look deep." She eyed Hunter up and down. "Use those butterfly bandages. Put plenty of antibiotic ointment on there. We don't want an infection."

Jillian watched the woman hover and fret, then fuss and demand. She couldn't tell if Della nurtured a modicum of compassion, or if she just liked being in charge. Either way, it was clear that Della was unwell and needed psychological help. For now, though, Jillian was glad that Della was allowing Hugh to get the help he needed, rudimentary as it would be out in the woods.

Hunter ministered to Hugh with care and competence, talking to him the whole time.

When he finished, Della asked, "Is he all right?"

Hunter turned to her. "From the wound on his head, yes, although he might have a concussion. And he might need X-rays to make sure nothing is broken." He glanced at Hugh, who said nothing but sat perfectly still, watching and listening.

"We are *not* going to the hospital, if that's what you've got in mind," Della said.

"But—" Hunter started to protest, but Della pointed the pistol straight at his chest. Always unflappable, he frowned as if the gun were nothing but a nuisance. "If anything happens to Hugh, it's all on you. You know that, right?"

Della pursed her lips and said nothing.

"How long have you kept him tied up?" Hunter asked.

Della narrowed her eyes. "I don't see how that's any of your business."

"Maybe not, but if you keep someone immobile for a prolonged period, it can cause problems, like blood clots. It's especially dangerous in an older person."

"He's not that old. No older than me."

Hunter scowled. "Young or old, a person needs to move around."

"I haven't kept him tied to the chair all this time we've been here, if that's what you mean. After I give him his sleeping pill and he gets drowsy, I untie him. He's not going anywhere when he's snoring away." Della made an airy gesture with one hand and gave a little laugh.

"Don't worry about me." Hugh spoke up, surprising them all.

"I need a bath and a shave, and a fresh change of clothes, but I'm doing okay. We've been walking outside to get a bit of exercise."

Jillian craned her head to stare at Hugh. *Is he actually defending the woman?* "Oh yeah?"

"Out in the front there in the mornings, before it gets too hot," Hugh said. "I've found Maudie's old flower beds. Lots of the perennials are still growing here and there in that scrub, all scraggly and sad. They're nearly fifty years old. One day, maybe we'll come back out here and . . ." His voice trailed off, and his brow furrowed. He looked down at the floor and murmured, "But maybe Maudie and I will never see this cabin together again. I don't know."

"You don't have to carry on like you're being mistreated, Hughie," Della said. "It never would have come to this if you had cooperated with me when I first asked you."

Jillian's attention sharpened. "Asked him what?"

Della ignored her as she sat down on the only other chair in the room. She closed her eyes for a moment, then popped them open and cast a sharp gaze at the others. "You people just sit there, be quiet, and let me think."

In a silence broken only by the sounds summer insects, twittering birds, and Roscoe panting from his place beside Jillian, the hot air inside the cabin grew more oppressive with every moment. The isolation bore down into Jillian's mind like a hornet. Her mouth and throat were dry.

Della drew in a deep breath and turned her attention to Hunter. "You go outside and wash up. You'll find a basin, some soap, and a towel next to the well. And give your girl a drink before you go out there. And fill that dog's water dish. It's no fun being thirsty in this heat."

Hunter poured Jillian a cup of water from the plastic jug on the table. He held it to her lips as she drank. It was tepid, but it slaked her thirst and she was grateful. "Thank you."

Della regarded her for a few seconds, then shot a glance to Hunter. "Don't dawdle. Go on now. I don't want germs around me. You do know how to draw water from a well, don't you?"

"I know how to use one," Hunter said. "When I was a kid, we had friends who owned a little place without running water in the house. It wasn't convenient, but it was educational."

Jillian listened in near horror. Why was Hunter talking to Della so casually, almost friendly, as if this were a simple, neighborly visit?

"Good. Take this." Della handed Hunter an empty plastic water jug. "Fill it while you're out there, would you?"

"Sure. Shall I top off that one too?" Hunter dipped his head toward the half-full container on the table.

"Why, yes, thank you." Della gave him a quick smile. "But wash up first. Don't bring any germs back in with you."

"No ma'am, I won't." He shot a glance at Jillian that spoke volumes she failed to understand. Then he went outside.

What had that look meant? And why on earth was he acting so amiable? Wasn't he worried? Didn't he understand that Della wasn't sane, and she could shoot all three of them out here in this forsaken place and get away with it?

Or did he know something Jillian didn't?

18

Della stood at the window and watched Hunter as he followed her orders. Jillian's nose itched and a trickle of sweat ran down her backbone. She squirmed in her restraints, wondering what was going to happen and when. She glanced at Hugh. He sat on the bed, leaning his back against the headboard, staring at nothing.

Had the pair's reunion reignited old feelings? Had he brought Della out here for a rendezvous and it turned into a hostage situation? Despite her fleeting belief earlier that Hugh and Della were at the cabin for a tryst, Jillian now refused to believe that Hugh would do such a thing. Something darker and more malevolent had clearly occurred. What did Hugh know about his ex-fiancée and singing partner? Was something like this the reason he had avoided Farris and Della for more than fifty years? Jillian yearned to fire these questions at him, but right then was neither the time nor place. She turned her attention to Della.

"What did you mean when you said you asked Hugh something he refused to do?" Jillian asked once more, as quietly and calmly as she could.

"If I wanted you to know, missy, I would have told you the first time you asked me, wouldn't I?"

Hugh met Jillian's gaze and shook his head. She took that to mean she should let the subject drop. She wanted answers, but Hugh was much better acquainted with this woman than Jillian was. He probably knew the scope of Della's actions and reactions. Jillian decided to trust him, and she didn't ask again.

"That's a good man you have there," Della said unexpectedly, still observing Hunter from the window.

Jillian was surprised at the woman's sudden change of tone. "Yes, he is."

"You'd best hang on to him. It's not easy to find a good man. In fact, it never has been easy." Della fell silent, then added, as if talking to herself, "I'm practically an expert." She looked at Hugh, who avoided her gaze. "I've made a lot of mistakes in my life."

"You know, holding us hostage is one of them." The words slipped from Jillian's mouth before she had time to consider them. She winced and bit her lip.

Instead of rounding on her and flourishing the pistol, Della carefully placed the gun in the deep pocket of her yellow caftan and opened a nearby overnight bag. She took out a tarnished silver hairbrush and went to the open front door, where a hot breeze stirred the folds of her garment. She pulled the brush slowly through her silvery-blonde tresses. The strands caught the light and gave her an almost ethereal glow.

Was Della really letting her guard down? Perhaps Hunter's gentle approach and respectful tone had reassured her, softened her. If Jillian were to follow his example, maybe she could discover a way out of this situation. It couldn't hurt to try.

"Your hair is lovely, Della." She forced herself to smile when the woman glanced over her shoulder in surprise.

"You think so?" Della asked.

"Such a beautiful color and texture."

Della turned from the door, her smile lighting up her face. "Thank you. It's been years and years since anyone has admired my hair."

Jillian felt she might be on the right track and dove in a little deeper. "I'm sure many have admired it but simply didn't say so aloud."

"Maybe. I suppose the reason no one tells me I'm beautiful anymore is because I'm older. Farris hardly notices me anymore." She stared down at the brush in her hand and sighed. Her expression turned soft and wistful. "I used to get compliments all the time, from everyone."

"I'm sure you did." Jillian ran her gaze along the hip-length locks. "Your hair is so long, I can't help but wonder if you have ever cut it."

Della laid the brush on the windowsill. Gathering the tresses into one hand, she pulled them over her shoulder and began to braid them without looking at what she was doing.

"When I was little," she said, "my mother hated my hair. It has always been thick and curly but very fine, so it tangled easily."

Jillian nodded. "I'm sure it did. My hair was the same way. It still is."

"I absolutely hated shampoo day. And so did my mother. I cried while she washed it, and then when she brushed out the snarls, I'd scream my head off."

"I can imagine," Jillian said. "My hair isn't nearly as lovely as yours. But it's curly and wayward with a mind of its own. It caused my mom and me plenty of trouble when I was growing up. It still does, actually. It hardly ever stays in the style I put it, even with hairspray."

"I hope your mother was gentler than mine." Della had reached the end of the braid and quickly secured it with a band. "Was she?"

"She tried to be. She'd spray on something that was supposed to detangle it, but that product never did live up to what its advertisements promised. Still, I guess using that was better than using nothing."

"I wish there had been some kind of product like that when I was a girl. It's good your mother didn't want to hurt you. Mine would yank the brush through my hair as if she was angry at me for growing it. Sometimes, I thought she might pull out every strand by the root."

Jillian felt a hard pang in her heart for the little girl who'd had to go through such treatment. "That's terrible."

"And of course, every morning, I'd wake up to a tangled mess," Della continued. "If she had braided it before bedtime back then—the way I've learned to do since—it wouldn't have gotten so knotted up while I slept. And I suppose I was a restless sleeper." Her hands stilled for a moment, and her eyes took on the expression of one who was lost in an ugly memory she could never forget. "One day she got her sewing shears out of the mending basket and lopped it all off."

"Oh no!"

"Oh yes. Every strand, as close to the scalp as she could. That was dreadful. My hair looked so bizarre that when I saw myself in the mirror, it terrified me. I still have nightmares about it."

"That's terrible, Della. I'm so sorry that happened to you."

"I don't think Mother intended to go that far. In an effort to fix it, she took me to my father's barber and told him to give me the same haircut he'd give any boy my age." She stared at her hands. "And he did."

"What a horrible thing to do to a little girl," Hugh said, drawing both their attentions. "You never told me about that, Del."

"Why should I have told you about it? I didn't want to put that image in your mind." Della gave Hugh a soft smile, then turned back to Jillian. "By the time I was old enough to take care of my hair myself, I never let a pair of scissors touch it again."

"I don't blame you." Jillian glanced at Hugh, whose pallor bothered her. The bruise on his forehead was dark with a knot growing beneath it. "Hugh, are you feeling all right? Della, he doesn't look well." She wished she could go to him, make him comfortable. She really, *really* wished she could get him out of that hot cabin and back to Moss Hollow where he belonged.

"I'm okay," he said. "Just a little hot, and my head hurts quite a bit."

"You need a drink of water, Hughie?" Della asked.

"Yes, if you don't mind."

"If you can wait until Jillian's boyfriend comes in with fresh water from the well, it'll be colder."

"I can wait."

"You're not running a fever, are you?" Jillian asked.

"I don't think so, but who can tell?" Hugh asked. "It's hotter than blue blazes in here."

Della walked over and laid her palm lightly against his forehead. He winced, and she patted his shoulder. "I don't believe you have a fever, and I can't do a thing about the weather, but I can dampen a cloth for you. Here's Hunter now. I'll get you a nice cool drink."

Hunter stepped into the house, the guitar under his arm and a water jug in both hands. He cast a glance around the room as if confused by what he saw there. If Jillian had not been tied up, she, Della, and Hugh could have been three friends having a friendly conversation. Hunter met her eyes in a silent question, but she said nothing, not wanting to alarm Della.

"Thank you," Della said as she took one of the water containers from Hunter. She got a red plastic cup and filled it for Hugh. "Here you go, hon. Can you hold it, or do you need some help?"

"I can handle it, thanks."

"Are you hungry?" she asked as he drank.

He lowered the cup. "A little, yes."

"Here, let me get you some more water." Della refilled the cup and handed it back. "What about you two?" She turned to Hunter and Jillian, smiling as if she were hosting a dinner party.

Although Jillian was grateful that Della seemed to be in a better mood, the gun still in her pocket made her far too anxious to think about food. Della's attitude shift had been so sudden that Jillian didn't trust it to last. She wanted to keep the woman calm, so being affable and courteous seemed to be the best course of action. "Just another nice cool glass of water for me, please."

"You do look a little hot and uncomfortable still. How about you, Hunter? We have apples and chips. We have plenty of mixed nuts, some rice crackers. There's peanut butter and jelly. And bread—gluten free, of course. I'm gluten intolerant, you know. I'm sorry we don't have a way of keeping things cold, so no meat or salads."

"That's fine," Hunter said. "But I guess it means we'll have no ice cream for dinner?"

She froze for a moment, then laughed. "Sorry, no."

"That's okay. I like peanut butter and jelly sandwiches," he said.

"Apple and peanut butter hits the spot when you're hungry too," Hugh said. "Good thing we bought plenty."

Della eyed the guitar as Hunter started to lean it against the wall. "Is it broken?"

"I don't believe so." He held it out to her.

She tipped her head toward Hugh. "That's his baby. Let him check it out."

"It's a little scratched up," Hunter said, handing it over.

Hugh accepted the instrument and examined it. "Those are old scratches."

Della regarded the guitar tenderly, started to say something, then turned away and began to lay out food.

Hugh ran his hand over the guitar. He examined the neck and the strings, touched the tuning pegs, frowned at the body and winced at the one place that seemed freshly damaged.

"Is it broken?" Jillian asked.

"A little split here on the back." Hugh's brow furrowed as he regarded the spot and ran the tip of his index finger over it. "It doesn't look too bad. Maybe it can be repaired."

"I didn't even know you could play a guitar until we walked up earlier and heard you." Jillian did her best to keep her tone conversational.

Hugh lifted his gaze and smiled at her. "It's been a long spell since I've played. I'm a little rusty."

"You wiped the rust off your abilities pretty quick," Della said over her shoulder. "Hugh can play any instrument you put in front of him."

"You can?" Jillian asked him in astonishment.

He shot a glance at Della's back while she worked. His expression was inscrutable, and Jillian wondered what was going on in his mind. He caught Jillian studying him and returned his attention to the guitar.

"Try it out," Jillian said. "See if it's okay."

"I'd rather—"

"Play 'Take My Heart,'" Della said.

"I don't—"

Della whirled around, her face rapidly changing from placid to stormy. "And play it bluesy. Like I've told you a thousand times already."

Jillian wished she hadn't asked him to play anything. "Della, Hugh's head probably hurts, and playing the guitar might make it worse."

"It never did before," Della snapped. "Play it, Hugh. Bluesy."

He shrugged, played a chord or two and turned the tuning pegs. When he plucked the strings, the sound wasn't as pure as it had been earlier, but the tune was sweet, sad, and, as Della had demanded, bluesy.

"That's lovely," Jillian said when he stopped.

"Thanks, but this split in the back has warped the sound, I'm afraid." Hugh frowned at the crack.

"That song right there will be a big hit," Della said as she brought the food to them. "As soon as we get it and a couple of others finished, we'll head to Nashville and record them."

There was a brief silence as she handed Hugh and Hunter

paper plates loaded with a variety of snack foods.

"You sure you don't want anything, Jillian?" she asked.

Hunter cleared his throat softly, drawing Jillian's attention. He gave her a nearly imperceptible nod.

"Actually, I *am* a little hungry," she said, although she wondered if she'd be able to swallow a single bite. "Maybe a few crackers."

"All righty," Della sang out.

Jillian had known many strange people in her life, but never anyone who inspired quite the same uneasy tingle of anxiety as Della Honeycutt. She may have been acting completely friendly right then, but what might she do in the next five minutes?

Hugh and Hunter didn't seem to feel the same sense of dread as Jillian. Had neither one heard Della's announcement about going to Nashville with her captives? Did it not seem as outlandish to them as it did to her? Maybe the men knew something she didn't. Maybe this day would end far better than it had started.

But how?

19

Jillian pondered the best way to follow Hunter's lead and soften up Della. Music seemed to be a wise choice. "You said you wrote that song?" Jillian asked.

"Yes ma'am," Della said proudly. "We wrote it together a long time ago." She returned to the food, placing crackers on another paper plate. "But we never got a chance to record it."

"I liked it very much."

"Did you?" Della smiled at her. "The tune was mostly Hugh's doing. The lyrics were mostly mine. I've added to them over the years, changed them a bit. I think it'll be a big hit."

"Maybe you could sing it for us. I'd like to hear it." Jillian couldn't believe she was encouraging her kidnapper to sing for her, but she'd try whatever she could to get things going their way.

Della held the plate, her round cheeks flushed and pretty. "I'd like that. We need to try it out on an audience before we take it to a producer, don't we, Hugh?"

"We need practice." Hugh glanced up from his plate and Jillian noted a spark of something new in his eyes. "Say, Del, how do you expect our gal to eat or drink when she's all tied up that way?"

Della gave him a blank stare as if she had forgotten Jillian was tied up, but then she seemed to remember. "Goodness, I don't know. I guess I should feed her. Or Hunter can."

"Hunter's eating." Whatever Hugh had in mind, Jillian was sure their freedom and safety was uppermost in his mind. "And she looks mighty uncomfortable."

"Are you uncomfortable when you're in the chair, Hughie?" Della asked.

"I am. Hot and miserable."

"Miserable?"

He nodded. "Like Hunter said, it's not good to keep someone where they can't move."

Della twisted her mouth as she pondered this. "You know, Hughie, the only reason I tie you to a chair is so you'll stay and help me with our music."

"I can help you without being tied to a chair." Hugh's voice was gentle and reassuring.

Nevertheless, Della snapped, "You never have before. As many times as I've asked you, pleaded and begged for you to come back to me so we can have our career, you've turned me down. Flat and firm every time."

"I have a life in Moss Hollow now. And a wife. I have for fifty years."

Della plunked down the plate she had been preparing for Jillian. "You weren't married fifty years that first Christmas I called you. You'd only been married a few months. And all these years since then, I've given you every opportunity to make it big, but you turned me down flat so you could hammer nails into someone else's house." Her eyes filled with tears. "All I wanted was my chance to make it, not to waste this voice God gave me."

"You didn't need me," Hugh said. "You could have done it on your own talent, Del."

"No I couldn't!" She sank to the floor and sat among the cracker crumbs, sobbing. "I let your brother sweet-talk me into marrying him instead of you. Oh, the promises he made, the dreams he offered. But after we got married, he dragged me from pillar to post, so all I had a chance to do was wash dishes or sweep floors for other women. He didn't want me to share my talent with the world, and he knew if you and I ever met up again, we'd get back together and make it big."

"That wouldn't have happened." Hugh set his plate aside on the bed and leaned forward. "I met Maudie. I fell in love with her, and I married her. I would never leave her for anyone or anything."

"You don't get it," Della cried. "I want my chance in Nashville. I never intended to take you away from Maudie."

"But, Della, you did take me away from her. And you did it at gunpoint," Hugh said. "There's no chance for us in Nashville. Even if we were to record a song, it would be a novelty. A one-hit wonder. That stardom you never achieved can't be reached with me. Not now."

"How can you say that? We have what it takes!"

"*Had*, Della. We *had* what it takes. Youth, strength, time. The years have taken those things from us and used them in other ways."

"No," she whimpered. "No, no, no." Della buried her face in her hands and bawled like a child, her body heaving.

Jillian couldn't staunch the sympathy that rose inside her and made her yearn to comfort the broken woman before her. A moment later, though, that tender feeling gave way to fear as Della blindly fumbled for her pocket and pulled out the pistol.

Hugh and Hunter froze. Hunter raised his eyes briefly to Jillian, then all three pinned their attention on Della. She held the pistol loosely, tears flooding her face, dripping from her cheeks and chin. She stared at the gun as if she'd never seen it before. She ran the tip of her index finger back and forth over the barrel, then lifted it to eye level. She tipped her head to one side and studied the grip. She touched the trigger, and Jillian held her breath. Della sighed and turned the gun so that it pointed at Hugh.

"No!" Jillian screamed. Roscoe sat up and barked.

Della jumped with surprise and dropped the pistol. It skittered across the floor, and both men dove after it. Hunter got to it first and held it aloft.

"It's not real!" Della shrieked, falling to her knees. She continued pleading and crying, her once soft and kind face now a tearstained mess.

Jillian's blood pounded in her ears so loudly that she could hardly hear the woman's words. It didn't help that Roscoe was barking sharply.

"What do you mean, it's not real?" Hugh shouted above the racket.

Hunter examined the pistol closely, then handed it him. "It's a toy. Very realistic, but a fake." He hurried to Jillian. He untied the nylon rope and found a paring knife in a kitchen drawer to cut the zip ties. She nearly cried with relief. As it was, she was weak from her head to her toes and swayed when she stood.

"Take it slow and easy, then move around," Hunter said. "Shake your arms and legs. Flex your hands. Get your circulation going."

She took his advice, but the day's fearsome events had sapped much of her physical strength.

Hugh was trying to get Della on her feet but having no luck. He straightened. "Can you get her up from the floor, Hunter? I'll see to Jillian."

"Is that okay?" Hunter asked her.

Jillian nodded. "Sure. I'll be fine in a minute."

He kissed her forehead, then turned to the woman on the floor.

Hugh came to Jillian's side and he pulled her into a warm, comforting embrace. "I'm so sorry you got dragged into this mess," he said softly. "I had no idea anything like this would happen, ever."

Jillian suddenly felt weaker and less able to help herself than she had when she was tied up. As hot as she was, she shivered and clung to Hugh. How odd that the man who'd been kept captive for a few days was able to give her strength when she'd been bound only an hour or so.

"You come outside with me," Hugh said. "We'll take it slow and easy. Roscoe, come."

He grabbed a few wrapped crackers and slipped them into his

pocket. With the puppy behind them, he led Jillian outside, where twilight was creeping in. After the close heat of the cabin, the outdoor air was fresh against her face and sweet going into her lungs.

At the well, Hugh filled a little tin cup with fresh cold water and gave it to her. "Don't gulp it. Savor it."

She did as he instructed, closing her eyes and sending up a thankful prayer. Once she caught her breath and realized the danger was over, she opened her eyes and glanced at Hugh, who was pouring water over a small towel. "How did this happen, Hugh? Whatever made you bring her out here in the first place?"

He raised both bushy gray eyebrows and handed Jillian the towel. "That ought to cool you off a bit." His bruised forehead looked even worse in the dusk that crept across the landscape. He stared into nothing for a moment, then met her gaze and answered her question. "You saw that pistol. *That* is what made me bring her out here."

"It wasn't because you wanted to be alone with her?" Jillian sponged her hot face with the cool towel, and it felt heavenly.

His eyes grew big and he stared at her, clearly appalled. "Of course not. What would give you an idea like that?"

"You were seen together early Thursday morning, and that's the last time anyone saw you."

Hugh shook his head. "I got up early, like I always do. That morning, Della was up before me, bustling around in the kitchen. She said she wanted to get their things together before they left and asked if I would take her to the store so she could buy a few snacks for their trip home. She said she didn't feel safe, going out alone in a strange town. I told her no one would bother her in Moss Hollow, but she was adamant. So I left Maudie a note in case she got up before we got back, and I drove Della to Food for Less. We bought some fruit and snacks and suchlike, and later, when I pulled out of the parking lot and onto the highway, she took that pistol out of her purse and ordered me to bring her here."

"My goodness." Jillian's breath caught in her chest. "Weren't you scared?"

"Sure I was. You saw the size of that thing. And how could I know it wasn't real? I did what she said, hoping at some point I could talk some sense into her."

"So she told you to come here? To this cabin?"

"Right."

"I've known you and Maudie forever, but I never knew you had this property. How did Della know about it?"

He drew down the corners of his mouth. "Like a knucklehead, I mentioned the place during Sunday dinner. Maudie was already upset with Della by then, and I was just talking, trying to distract her."

"Oh my." Jillian recalled all the unkind notions that she'd pondered about this good man, and guilt roiled in her stomach.

"You don't look so good," he said. "Come over here and sit down."

He led her to a place where the grass was lush and soft. She sat down and Roscoe bounded into her lap. He nuzzled against her, his small body quivering as she stroked him gently.

Hugh fetched her another cup of water from the well and settled down beside her while she sipped. "You thought I ran off with Della, didn't you?" he asked.

"It crossed everyone's mind."

He winced. "Even Maudie?"

She took another sip and nodded. "Especially Maudie."

"What about the note I left her? Didn't she get that?"

Jillian shook her head. "I don't think she did. Maybe Della found it and threw it away before you left the house."

"Seems likely." Hugh sighed. "I'm not too surprised everyone else could think such an ugly thing, given how scandals seem to be the preferred topic of conversation everywhere these days." He blew out another huge breath and shook his head sorrowfully. "I guess I understand why Maudie *might* believe that, but she should know I'd never leave her. Not on purpose, and not for someone else. Especially someone like Della."

"You and Della did seem pretty chummy, especially at the party."

"You've met her. It's best to keep her happy."

"And keeping your family secret from everyone, including your wife, gave the rumor mill plenty of grist."

"All that with Farris and Della was an embarrassing event in my life, and I saw no reason to share it. It was in the past. I didn't want to let it tarnish this wonderful life I've built with Maudie." Hugh pulled up a few blades of grass. "I don't understand why Farris thought it was a good idea to try to reconnect."

"He seems to want nothing more than to make amends." Jillian took another sip of water.

"Make amends? Farris?"

"For hurting you the way he did."

"You mean because they eloped a few days before Della and I were supposed to be married? He did me a favor, if you want the truth."

"Then why haven't you forgiven him?"

He gave her an odd look. "Who says I haven't?"

Jillian cocked her head at him. "You mean you have?"

"Sure. A long time ago. Like I said, he did me a favor. If I'd married Della, she would have driven me crazy. And more importantly, I'd never have met Maudie."

Jillian studied the face of this kind man she had known all her life. She had never seen any deception in him, and she saw none now. "Then why did Farris say—"

Hugh shook his head. "My brother is a compulsive liar. He spins the most outrageous yarns and tells them in such a way that people believe him. He makes promises he'll never keep. I wanted to get away from that. And I sure didn't want Maudie to be exposed to it, so I never brought the two of them together. She's very trusting and sees the best in folks, which is one of the things I love most about her. But with Farris, it could get her into trouble."

"I can understand that."

"If she'd known I had a brother, she'd have done just what she did a few weeks ago—insist that we all get together. I had to protect her from that. You understand why I kept my secret, don't you?"

"I do. But you'll need to explain it to her."

"I will." He gazed at the cabin, and a gentle smile curved his lips. "That was my idea. The cabin. I thought it would be a nice little place for us to get away from the world, be alone for a day or two whenever we wanted. I bought it for next to nothing, put in a new roof, reinforced the interior, built that porch, and replaced the flooring. When I brought Maudie out here that first bright warm Saturday in June 1975 . . ." His voice trailed off and his gaze drifted, taking in the landscape that surrounded them.

"What did she say?" Jillian prompted gently.

Hugh's face broke into a soft smile. "She was so good about it. She praised the work I'd done and talked about how quiet and pretty it was out here in the woods. I should have known this rustic cabin in the middle of nowhere wasn't her cup of tea. We came back a few times, but she likes being around people. She likes the sound of neighbors, likes to see them coming and going, likes to go shopping or visiting." He met Jillian's eyes. "I guess I bought this cabin for me instead of us. And you know something? Without Maudie, there *is* no us. I like country living, but I'd rather spend my days with her, even if we moved to a high-rise in the city."

Jillian reached up and brushed away a lone tear that strayed from her eye. "You're a good man, Hugh."

Hunter stepped out of the cabin then, one arm around Della's shoulders to steady her, his free hand holding onto one of hers. As he guided her down the steps, he looked at Hugh and Jillian. "We're ready to go home," he said quietly.

The Southern Sweetie Pies filled the second-floor waiting room at the Nathan County Hospital. Instead of gathering at The Chocolate Shoppe, they had chosen to move that Sunday's meeting a little closer to Wanda Jean.

Although the patient was in a pink robe and matching slippers, her hair was in its usual neat bun. She wore a touch of blush and lipstick, but it was her huge smile that made her seem like her old self. Seated in the wheelchair that an orderly had brought her out in, Wanda Jean talked and laughed with her dear friends for nearly an hour before a nurse poked her head into the room and told them all they had five minutes left.

"It appears we've about overstayed our welcome," Bertie said, gathering her purse and gesturing for the others to do so as well. "You take care of yourself, Wanda Jean. You're looking good."

"I'm feeling good," Wanda Jean said. "And I'll be home in a day or two. You all come to see me there, okay? I won't have a nurse chasing you away."

Hugh and Maudie lingered behind as the rest of the Sweetie Pies filed toward the elevator. Jillian thought she hadn't seen them more than half an inch apart since they'd reunited with unabashed joy the night before at Belle Haven.

"Are you two lovebirds coming?" Cornelia asked from the doorway.

Maudie waved them ahead. "They're going to let us see her alone for a bit. We'll be back to Belle Haven soon."

"We appreciate you letting us stay for a little while, ladies," Hugh said.

"It'll give the cleaning crew a chance to get rid of any trace of those . . . those . . ." Maudie let her words trail off before she said anything else.

"If you don't mind me saying, Hugh, I think it's noble of you not to press charges against that woman," Cornelia said airily.

Hugh made a dismissive gesture. "Della doesn't need jail. She needs someone to help her work through her problems. My brother promised to get her the care she needs back in Wyoming. I've never believed much of what he's pledged to do, but I do think he loves her and wants to do right by her."

"It's mighty decent of you either way," Bertie said. "Now you two go on back and have your chat with Wanda Jean. I'm sure you have plenty to catch up on, having barely spoken in five whole days." Bertie delivered the last line with a wink, then headed for the elevator.

"You two take your time getting back to Belle Haven," Cornelia said as she followed Bertie out of the room.

Maudie caught Jillian's arm before she could follow her great-aunt and grandmother. "Jillian, wait."

Jillian stopped. "Yes, Maudie?"

"I just wanted to—I mean, I—thank you." Maudie pulled Jillian into a tight embrace. "You're a true friend."

"I didn't do anything anybody else wouldn't have done," Jillian said.

"You didn't believe the worst about Hugh, even when I fooled myself into thinking it, and that means almost as much to me as you rescuing him."

Jillian smiled at the couple. "You two are the real deal. You have been for fifty years. Not everyone is so lucky."

"I think you might be, dear," Maudie said with a knowing look. "Now come on, Hugh. You can watch the Braves game while Wanda Jean and I catch up."

Jillian's cell phone rang as she watched the Honeycutts walk down the hall, arm in arm. She smiled when the screen told her who was calling.

"Hi, Hunter," she said brightly. "I was just thinking about you."

Trifling With Trouble
Book Twenty One Recipe

Bertie's Coconut Cream Cake

Cake

½ cup margarine, softened
½ cup shortening
2 cups sugar
5 eggs, separated
1 teaspoon baking soda
1 cup buttermilk

2 cups cake flour
1 cup shredded coconut
1 teaspoon vanilla
½ cup chopped pecans
(optional)

Frosting

8 ounces cream cheese,
softened
¼ cup margarine or butter,
softened

1 teaspoon vanilla
4 cups confectioners' sugar
Shredded coconut for garnish
Chopped pecans (optional)

Directions

1. Preheat oven to 350. Grease and flour three 8-inch or two 10-inch round cake pans.

2. Using a stand or hand mixer, cream margarine and shortening together. Add sugar gradually, continuing to cream into the margarine and shortening until combined.

3. Add egg yolks one at a time, beating well after each one. Place egg whites in a separate large mixing bowl.

4. Combine baking soda and buttermilk. Slowly beat buttermilk mixture into the sugar mixture alternately with flour. Add coconut and vanilla. Add pecans if desired.

5. Beat egg whites until stiff peaks form. Gently fold beaten egg whites into batter.

6. Divide batter equally between pans and bake for 25 to 30 minutes, or until a toothpick inserted in the center comes out clean. Cool on rack.

7. To make frosting, cream together cream cheese and margarine. Add vanilla and stir until combined. Beat in confectioners' sugar 1 cup at a time until desired sweetness and consistency are reached. Frost and assemble cooled cake layers. Top with shredded coconut and pecans (if desired).

Up to this point, we've been doing all the writing. Now it's *your* turn!

Tell us what you think about this book, the characters, the bad guy, or anything else you'd like to share with us about this series. We can't wait to hear from *you*!

Log on to give us your feedback at:
https://www.surveymonkey.com/r/ChocolateShoppe

Annie's® FICTION

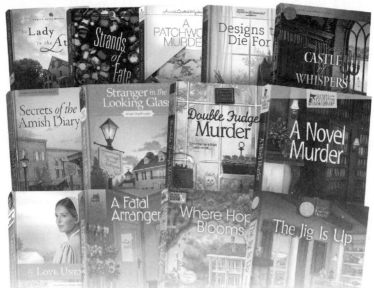